KEVIN DAVID ANDERSON'S

NIGHT OF THE ZOMBEES

A Zombie Novel with Buzz!

Also by

KEVIN DAVID ANDERSON

Night of the Living Trekkies (with Sam Stall)

Blood, Gridlock, and PEZ: Podcasted Tales of Horror

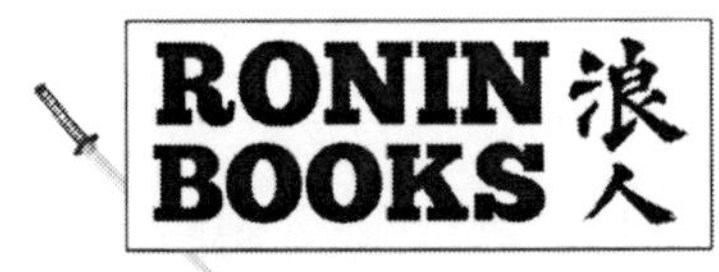

Cover art and design by Bo Kaier
Instagram @bokaier | www.bokaier.com

ISBN-13: 978-0615916781
ISBN-10: 0615916783

To Avalon and Ronin
Be brave, laugh often, and run fast!

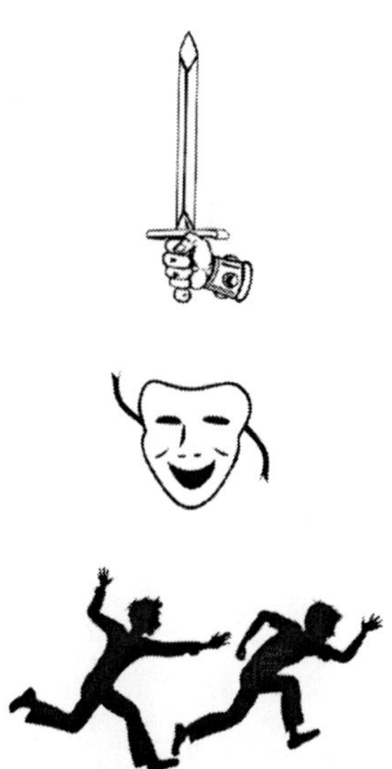

"I think people that love the genre giggle at it.
I don't get grossed out, I giggle."
— George A. Romero

"Never say 'no' to adventures. Always say 'yes'
otherwise you'll lead a very dull life."
— Ian Fleming

CHAPTER

1

NEVER DREAM OF DYING

They were coming for him again, thousands of them.

Diving from the sky like mini-fighter planes, their syringe-length stingers targeted his young frame. Shaun knew thrashing would only make it worse, but he couldn't stop himself. With his heart pounding, he slapped at the attacking bees, crushing each tiny creature moments after delivering its piercing sting. Every needle-like puncture sent a bolt of pain up his spine. He wanted to run, but the insects covered his face, and he had to close his eyes. The swarm's weight pulled him down, and his knees buckled.

Shaun dropped, then started to roll, hoping to crush them on the ground. But for every one he smashed, a hundred more seemed to drop from the sky. The pinpricks of pain spread like fire, and Shaun couldn't tell what part of his body had been stung and which hadn't. He screamed but all he could hear was buzzing.

Then a distant voice cut through the hail of swarming insects. "Shaun…"

Someone's coming for me, Shaun thought. He couldn't see who, but the shouting of his name was getting louder.

"Shaun, Shaun," the voice yelled. "Wake up!"

Shaun's eyes popped open. He sat up so fast he tumbled from the stack of empty milk crates he'd dozed off on.

"I don't pay you to take naps!" roared Shaun's boss, Mr. Hooper.

Shaun scrambled to his feet, running his hands over his body, half expecting to find bees crawling underneath his clothes. *Just another dream. Will they ever end?*

"Now if you're not too busy, I have an order ready." Mr. Hooper's voice had gone from loud to sarcastic. "I'd be delighted if my *delivery boy* could stay awake long enough to do his job."

After a few blinks, the painful images of the dream were gone and Shaun now focused on the enormous man.

"Yes sir, I'm ready," Shaun said, standing up as straight as possible.

The grocery store manager put his hands on his wide hips and glared at Shaun. Mr. Hooper was a volcano-shaped man with a fiery lava flow of hair and burning hot eyes. Shaun hated those eyes. He could feel their heat constantly boring into him.

Mr. Hooper pointed at Shaun's bike, the weight of the groceries in the baskets causing it to lean precariously. "You're all loaded. Now get that delivery out to Dr. Romero ASAP, then hightail it back here for more."

Shaun wasn't sure what he was least excited about the most, having to deliver what looked like eight very heavy bags of groceries, or having to pedal them all the way out to Dr. Romero's house. The Doc was a good guy, friendly, but his monstrous house doubled as the doctor's laboratory. Every time Shaun went out there, the doctor invited him in for a peek at one of his experiments, all of which involved bees. Shaun had little interest in science and had seen enough bees to last several lifetimes. But he always pretended to enjoy the tour, smiled politely, and hoped for a good tip.

"Is there a problem?" Mr. Hooper said.

"Nothing," Shaun said, reaching into his pocket for his inhaler. He took a squirt of his asthma medicine.

Mr. Hooper gave Shaun a look he usually reserved for produce that has gone bad. "If this job is to much for you—"

"No, no," Shaun said. "I live to deliver groceries. It's my destiny."

"Don't get snarky with me, Shaun. I only gave you this job as a favor to your father."

"I know," Shaun said. "You mentioned that yesterday, and the day before that, and the day before that, and everyday since I started."

"I should never have hired a thirteen-year-old, and why aren't you wearing any black and yellow? You know what day this is."

Shaun was dressed as he was most days, in cut-off jeans, Tardis blue Converse high tops, and an oversized polo shirt a few shades darker than his sand-colored hair. "My mom made me a bee costume for the Founders Day Festival but it's kind of hard to wear on my bike." This wasn't true. Shaun's mom hadn't made him a bee costume since he was eight. She knew he'd never wear it.

"No employee of mine is going to be disrespectful and not show town spirit. Here in Honeywell Springs we dress up for Founders Day." He gestured to his own outfit, a bedazzled black-and-yellow-striped apron worn over a yellow button-down shirt and black tie. A pair of novelty bee antennas sprouted from his red hair. He looked ridiculous.

"I know, Mr. Hooper."

"If you aren't going to put on a bee costume, then at least wear some black and yellow."

Shaun was bored with this conversation, and he could pretend only so long to take seriously a man wearing metal springs with black fuzz-balls sprouting from his head.

Shaun snapped off a salute. "Yes, sir. I'll get right on it, sir. I live to serve, sir."

"Don't get smart."

"Yes, sir. Remaining dumb, sir."

"Just get back here by four, with a signed credit card receipt or I'll—"

"Dock my salary," Shaun finished. "You mentioned that yesterday, and the day before, and the day before that."

Mr. Hooper pointed his finger, his traditional wind-up gesture for a very long lecture about either responsibility, respecting elders, working hard, or Shaun's all-time least favorite, being a part of a community.

"Okay, gotta go now." Shaun hurried to his bike, talking over his shoulder. "Got groceries to deliver, receipts to get signed, black and yellow clothes to find, busy, busy."

Shaun jumped on his bike and pushed off without looking back. He didn't need to experience the heat from Mr. Hooper's disapproving gaze.

Is any video game worth this? Shaun had only taken this job so he could buy the next generation gaming console and the new incarnation of *Chopping Maul*, the video game he and his best friend Toby loved more than anything. Well, anything except for James Bond movies.

As he struggled to keep the overloaded bike steady, he wondered if James Bond ever had to spend his summer doing stupid delivery jobs. *Probably not.* The world's greatest secret agent probably had really cool jobs as a kid, like loading ammo into machine guns mounted under the hood of an MI-6 agent's Italian sports car, or installing the lasers on spy satellites, or maybe—

"Shaun!" From the other side of the parking lot, his friend Toby was waving his hands like an idiot, in clear view of Mr. Hooper.

Shaun gestured for him to stop but it did little good. Toby kept shouting as if Shaun couldn't hear him. Glancing back to see if Mr. Hooper was watching he was relieved to see that the big man was already stepping back inside, his black-and-yellow apron flapping like a superhero's cape on backwards.

Shaun rode over to Toby. "Dude, I told you to keep out of sight. If Mr. Hooper finds out you're helping me with my deliveries, he'll fire me. He already thinks I'm too young."

"Sorry, bro. No caddying today at the golf course, so I thought I'd just head over. Besides, I spied the coolest update on the GameWire forum and I'm way too excited."

"About?"

"They just announced the release date for *Chopping Maul 5: Black Friday*."

"We haven't even played version four yet."

"We're falling behind, bro."

Living in a small town like Honeywell Springs, Shaun always felt they were falling behind. The local theater played movies that had been out everywhere else for months, the arcade games at the bowling alley were from the 1990s, and the surrounding hills made cell phone reception hit or miss. It was like living on an island. A tiny, dull, black-and-yellow, bee-infested island. But having a friend like Toby somehow made it bearable.

Shaun and Toby had been best buds since kindergarten. Their friendship was built on a solid foundation of video games, junk food, and a fascination with James Bond. They'd watched each 007 flick at least ten times, and the movies had inspired them to make a pact.

When they were old enough they'd leave Honeywell Springs, enroll in spy school and become international secret agents. They would spend their lives going on dangerous missions, taking down global villains, and saving the world. But that was a long way off, and before they could do any of that, they'd have to get this delivery to Dr. Romero's house.

"Man, this is a lot of groceries," Toby said as Shaun transferred some of the bags to a basket designed to hold a set of golf clubs. "I think you should split the tip with me."

"Fine. How about we split it 20-80?"

Toby considered for a moment. "40-60, you fat cheapskate."

"30-70, ya mooch."

"Nah," Toby said. "Final offer, 60-70."

"What, dude? That doesn't even…" Shaun shook his head. "Oh, forget it. I'll give you half. I hate doing math in the summer."

Toby transferred another bag and Shaun took in Toby's black-and-yellow-striped sweater. It fit loosely under his thin face and jet-black hair. The stripes swirled around at an angle, making Toby's top half look like a bizarre barber's pole. His bottom half was equally strange but not out of the ordinary. Toby had gone from Wii golf to real golf three years ago, and what came with the new hobby was a collection of the ugliest pants ever created. Golf pants, which he even wore to school. The kids teased him but Toby never seemed to care. Today's golf trousers were turquoise, held up by a bone-white leather belt that looked like it should be on somebody's grandfather, not on a thirteen-year-old boy.

"Aren't you dying in that sweater?" Shaun handed Toby another bag. "It's like a hundred degrees."

"I know." Toby picked the sweater off his chest, fanning the air underneath. "My grandma made it, and if I don't wear this for Founders Day my mom is gonna make me put on the matching bee costume she got for the whole family this year."

"Matching?"

"The whole family, dude. Antennas, big old stinger hanging off the butt."

"That's harsh, man," Shaun said.

"Tell me about it. So where're we going?"

"Dr. Romero's house."

Toby's face lit up like a Christmas tree. "Sweet! I've always wanted to go out there."

"Why?" Shaun asked.

Toby grabbed another bag. "You always make it sound so cool."

"Not on purpose." Shaun said. The boys jumped on their seats and pushed off.

"Hey, you can't go that way," Toby said.

"Why not?"

Toby pulled alongside of him. "You know, Founder's Day. All of downtown is closed to traffic. They won't even let bikes through this year."

"Seriously?"

"No worries, bro," Toby said. "Follow me. We'll cut across the golf course."

Shaun followed, wondering how they would make it over the fairways without getting plugged by a golf ball. He was going to ask but by the time he reached his friend, Toby was going on about the festival.

"I scoped it out this morning. This year's is gonna be the sickest celebration ever. They brought in a carnival, Ferris wheel, carousel, dunk tank, carnie games. And everyone is in costume. Even the creepy carnies I saw had black and yellow on. Mayor Savini wants everyone to go all out for the VIPs this year. My dad said honey buyers are coming from Stein Mart, K-Mart, Wal-Mart, S-Mart, and a whole bunch of other *marts*."

Toby glanced over at Shaun, clearly trying to gauge his interest.

Shaun tried to show some by nodded politely.

"And all the sheriff's deputies," Toby continued, "are wearing these seriously heinous black-and-yellow uniforms, and a vest with a hoody that has antennas. My mom and the Ladies Auxiliary worked on them all month. I can't wait to see Sheriff Rosco in his. I'm gonna laugh my—" Toby looked over at Shaun. "Are you even listening?"

"Yes." Shaun flashed a halfhearted smile. "Sounds epic."

"So come to the festival this year, man."

Shaun shook his head and peddled faster, hoping to avoid his friend's gaze.

"Hey, what happened to you sucked, but it was years ago," Toby said. "Eventually you got to get over this thing with bees, man. I mean, you live in Honeywell Springs of all places, the honey bee capital of the world."

"I know where I live, fart-face."

"Just think of how awesome it would be making fun of all the grown-up tools in their bee getups. They'll all be in costume this year. Absolutely everyone. And it's tradition man."

"Dude, I've lived here my whole life. I'm aware of our ginormously lame hundred-year-old tradition."

The Founder's Day holiday, celebrating the tiny creatures that made the town possible had been Shaun's least favorite day since his nightmares began. Honeywell Springs had dozens of honey farms, three honey packaging factories, almost a hundred agricultural hive growers, and several companies that created products from honey and beeswax, such as medicines and ointments, most of which were invented by Dr. Romero. It was absolutely the worst place on the planet to live if you suffered from apiphobia. The fear of bees.

"Can you drop it?" Shaun snapped. "You're starting to sound like my mom."

"Fine, butt-nugget," Toby said. "But you need to get over—"

"Hey, we're here," Shaun interrupted loudly never so happy to see the entrance to the Honeywell Springs Golf Course just ahead. "So what's the plan?"

"We cut across the course," Toby said. "We head out to the back nine, then straight out of town. The doctor's place is only a mile or two from the course."

"But how do we ride our bikes on the course without getting chased off or beaned with a line drive?"

"Dude," Toby said. "It's Founders Day, the one day of the year the course is closed. We have the whole place to ourselves, man."

Shaun couldn't help but smile. "Genius, Toby. I knew there was a reason I liked you."

"There're lots of reasons why you like me."

"Not really."

"You like my sense of humor."

"Nope. You're not funny."

"My conversation?"

"I could live without it."

"My gaming skills are legendary."

"Yeah, legendarily weak."

"So's your face," Toby said.

Shaun chuckled. "What does that even mean?"

Toby rattled off more of his likable attributes as they rounded the clubhouse, zipped through the golf cart area, and headed straight for the back nine. They were cutting across the seventeenth green when Shaun heard something. It was distant but seemed to be getting closer— a high-pitched buzzing or whine. Shaun's heart quickened, and his lungs tightened. Hitting the brakes, he stopped in the middle of the fairway, in the shadow of a grass-covered cliff overlooking a sand trap.

Toby stopped beside him. "I always share my Twix bar with you."

"Shut up a minute," Shaun said. "You hear it?"

"What?"

"That buzzing."

"It's Honeywell Springs. There's *always* buzzing."

"But I—"

Something big zipped over the crest of the hill. A dark, ball-shaped mass rose into the sky with a thundering buzz, momentarily blocking the sun. It hung there for a beat then arced downward. Shaun realized that whatever it was, it was coming down fast. Right on top of them. They needed to move, but Shaun was frozen, paralyzed in the shadow engulfing him. Toby scrambled away but Shaun remained rooted to the spot. All he could do was raise his arms and brace for impact.

CHAPTER

2

THUNDERBALL

Buzzing like a chainsaw, the dark mass that dropped out of the sky clipped Shaun's handlebars with a forceful, metallic thud. Whatever it was crashed to the ground nearby, as Shaun fell back into the grass, his bike and bags of groceries falling on top of him.

Flat on his back, Shaun could see nothing but sky. Feeling the debris of groceries all around, he was suddenly grateful that golf isn't played on concrete, because if it were his head would be split open. He sat up slowly.

"What're you idiots doing out here?" a voice yelled.

Toby had managed to avoid the collision. He stood a few feet away, still on his bike.

"What're *you* doing here, riding that thing?" Toby fired back at someone Shaun couldn't see. "This is a PGA championship-ranked golf course, man!"

Shaun was about to stand up when something landed on his hand. *It's just a fly*, he thought. *Please, please, be a fly*. Shaun peered down. His heart began to pound and his lungs seized up. *Not a fly*.

The bee crawled over Shaun's knuckles then stopped, its feelers probing a vein on the top of his hand. Shaun needed to gasp for air, but his chest was locked. He stayed completely still, sweat trickling down his temple. The insect's abdomen twitched and its stinger emerged from the back as piercing as a sewing needle.

Something slapped the top of Shaun's hand, hard. He recoiled, his hand stinging, but not stung. He reached into his pocket and retrieved his inhaler. After a double-shot, his lungs relaxed.

Toby knelt down next to him. "You okay?"

Shaun took a breath and nodded.

Someone wearing a helmet loomed over them. "Geez, what's his damage?"

"He has a thing about bees," Toby said.

"Seriously?" A snort came from inside the helmet. "Man, does he live in the wrong town."

A round of laughter bubbled over the top of the hill. A half dozen kids, all wearing black-and-yellow shirts, sat on BMX bikes.

Shaun gazed up at the figure standing over him. The sun was behind the helmet, and Shaun couldn't see the face. But whoever it was wore a black *No Fear* t-shirt and dark shorts with the Monster Energy Drink logo on the sides. When the person pulled off the motorcycle helmet, crimson curls fell out, and Shaun recognized who it was.

Sam Campbell cradled the helmet on a hip and smirked. "What a dweeb."

Shaun felt a spark of anger as the kids laughed again. Sam wasn't the biggest bully in school, but definitely an up-and-comer. In third grade Sam dumped dirt down Shaun's shirt every day for a week, until Shaun finally worked up the nerve to tell a teacher. When Toby took up golf, Sam was always there to tease him about his choice of pants. Shaun had wanted to punch Sam at least a dozen times in the last few years, but he never did. For one, Shaun had never hit anyone in his life and if he tried, he'd probably do more damage to himself than who he was hitting. Second, the name Sam was short for Samantha, and no matter how much he thought she deserved it, Shaun would never hit a girl.

Toby found the bee and picked it up by one of its misshapen wings. "You killed it."

"So?" Sam said with a shrug.

"Don't you know it's illegal to kill a bee in Honeywell Springs?" Shaun said. He didn't really care that the bee was dead; he just didn't like being laughed at.

"You have a strange way of saying thank you, dork." Sam looked like she didn't give two snot-rockets about laws, rules, or riding her mini-motorcycle on a championship-rated golf course. "Losers." She rolled her eyes and turned to her small motorbike.

"Hey, Sam," called one of the kids on the hill. "It's getting late. The festival is gonna start."

Sam knelt next to her bike. The word *Thunderball* was emblazoned across the gas tank. "You, guys go ahead. I'll catch up."

"You, sure?" a kid yelled.

Sam waved a hand over her shoulder. "Later, dudes."

The kids zipped down the hill as Toby helped Shaun to his feet. Shaun assessed the damaged groceries.

Sam righted her bike. "Ah, man! The forks are bent." She let the bike fall to the ground and turned back to Toby and Shaun. "What the heck are you guys doing out here, anyway?"

Shaun picked up a bag that was leaking something and held it out to her. "I'm working. What're you doing, flying through the air on that death-machine?"

Sam pointed back up the hill. "I was trying to clear that monster sand trap. The one day of the year I could have totally crushed it, and you two dweebs have to be in the way."

"Sorry we got in the way of you trying to kill yourself," Shaun said, looking into the leaking bag. "But you now owe me a jar of dill pickles and…" Shaun tilted the bag so he could read the label of the other broken jar. "A jar of whatever the heck gefilte fish is."

"Well, you owe me a new mini-motorcycle," Sam snapped. "Why don't we just call it even?"

"Even," Shaun repeated. "You're not supposed to be out here."

"And you are?"

"She's got you there, man," Toby said.

Shaun glared at Toby. "Not helping, dude."

"Look, dweebs," Sam said, picking up her bike. "I could care less about your pickles and your weird fish." She rolled her bent bike over to them. "As far as the trespassing thing goes, you didn't see me, and I didn't see you. Just like at school." Sam held up a fist, looking very much like she knew how to use it. "Got it?"

Shaun and Toby stared at her knuckles, white and threatening.

"You have to admit," Toby said, "she makes a real good argument."

Shaun asked, "Whose side are you on?"

"The side that doesn't get us beat up."

"Fine," Shaun said, looking at Sam. "Neither of us were ever here."

"Whatever." Sam lowered her fist and moved away. "Hasta la vista, dweebs."

Shaun and Toby watched as Sam pushed her bike down the fairway toward the clubhouse. When she was out of earshot, Toby said, "Do you think Sam is kind of… you know, cute?"

Shaun stared at Toby. "Did she run over your head?"

"Come on," Toby said. "Take away the anger, the meanness, the black clothes and… you don't think she's a little cute?"

"I guess." Shaun sighed. "In the way baby Godzilla is cute. Now can we stop screwing around? We're late."

"Okay, Grouchy McGroucherson." Toby helped Shaun repack his bike and a few minutes later they were back on course. They continued cutting across the greens, then rode out onto Old Nectar Road. It was mostly dirt, very bumpy, but it was the only way out to Dr. Romero's house.

A half mile after they left the golf course, the road went through what Shaun thought was the creepiest part of the ride, a thicket of trees that rose up high and dense. The branches were so long and lush that they reached across the road, blocking most of the sky. It was like a natural tunnel, with walls of tree bark and a rustling ceiling of leaves.

Toby kept talking about Sam as they entered. "You don't think we had a little moment back there, Sam and I."

"What're you talking about?" Shaun said, noticing the temperature drop as the warm sunlight disappeared. "You hardly talked to her."

"No, it was more an unspoken thing," Toby said. "It was just a look between us."

"The only thing I saw between you and Sam was her fist, which she was about to beat us—" Shaun suddenly quit talking as a rumbling permeated the trees. Toby was listening too. His eyes were wide and cast upward. They stopped in the middle of the tree-formed tunnel, as the sound grew.

"What is it?" Toby said.

Shaun shook his head. "It's getting louder."

"Sounds like bees, but… different."

They scanned for beehives in the branches above.

The buzzing became a roar.

"It's not in the trees," Shaun said, his pulse racing. "It's above…"

Slivers of blue sky, visible through gaps in the leafy ceiling, flickered as dark forms streaked overhead. Shaun pulled out his inhaler, but before he could use it the roar from above began to fade. Whatever it was had moved off. Shaun and Toby remained still and quiet until the lingering echo of the monstrous buzz was completely gone.

When the only sound left was the breeze rustling the leaves, Toby looked at Shaun. "An airplane, maybe? Crop duster?"

Shaun pictured the dozens of flying murky shapes he'd glimpsed. "I don't think so."

"What, then?"

"I don't know, and I don't want to know," Shaun said. "I just want to drop this load off and get back before…" He looked at his watch. It was already four o'clock. He imagined Mr. Hooper standing at the back door of the store, fists on hips, waiting. "Before I get fired. Come on."

They peddled fast. Clearing the tree tunnel in less than a minute, Shaun and Toby huffed and puffed over the next rise. When they reached the crest they could just see the roof of Dr. Romero's house between the treetops. Shaun hoped the doctor wasn't in the mood to give them a tour, because if he didn't get back and do at least two more deliveries, this day would be a total loss.

During Shaun's last tour of Dr. Romero's laboratory the doctor showed Shaun his latest experiment, something to do with women's makeup; a skin cream made from bee venom that could generate human cells. Or was it regenerate dead cells? Shaun couldn't remember because he was too distracted by the horrific mutations the doctor had created. They scurried about in glass aquariums all around the lab. The glowing honey bee that had been genetically mixed with a firefly was interesting, but the African Killer Bee that the doctor combined with an arachnid was the stuff of nightmares. Dr. Romero called the oversized, creepy, half-bee, half-spider a Bumblebeeder, and the thought of it getting loose kept Shaun up at night.

Whatever unsettling thing the doctor insisted on showing Shaun, at least he wouldn't have to bear it alone. Besides, Toby loved horror movies and would probably think the flying eight-legged, black-and-yellow terror was cool.

"Is that the house?" Toby pointed at the two-story dark wood home.

"Dead ahead," Shaun said.

"It looks like the house in *Psycho*, man. So cool."

"Whatcho?"

"*Psycho.*"

"Horror movie?" Shaun asked.

Toby nodded. "Total classic, dude."

Shaun didn't care for horror movies. He liked horror in video games, where you could try to control the outcome. With movies it felt like he was just along for the terrifying ride, and that lack of control sometimes triggered his asthma.

As their tires rolled onto Dr. Romero's property, Shaun immediately felt that something was wrong. He'd never seen a car on the driveway, wasn't sure if the doctor even had one. Now there was not just one, but two vehicles parked outside.

Shaun and Toby stopped their bikes near the car by the rickety porch. It was a Honeywell County Sheriff's vehicle, and the driver's side door was open. Shaun peered inside. The interior light was on, but the car was empty. The shotgun rack on the dashboard was also empty.

Toby moved toward the other vehicle. "What kind of truck is this?" He peered in the back through its open rear doors.

"It says Animal Control on the side."

"Does Dr. Romero have a pest problem?" Toby asked.

The image of Dr. Romero's creature he called a Bumblebeeder popped into Shaun's thoughts. *Maybe it got loose.* Reaching back, he grabbed two of the heavy bags from the rear basket. "Come on. Let's drop this stuff and get out of here."

Toby followed him up the wooden steps. They stood shoulder to shoulder at the big door. Shaun shifted the bags to one hand so he could knock. When his knuckles hit the door, it swung inward, hinges creaking like a rusty mausoleum door unopened for centuries. Toby and Shaun looked at one another, then back into the big silent house.

Shaun knocked on the door frame. "Hello, Dr. Romero! It's Shaun. I've got your groceries."

No answer.

"Maybe he's upstairs," Toby said.

"Well, why don't you go and see?"

Toby motioned his hand inside. "After you."

"No, that's okay," Shaun said. "You go first."

Toby shook his head, repeating his hand gesture. "Not at all. Age before beauty."

"Dude, you're two months older than me."

"I didn't say what age," Toby said.

Shaun sighed. "Come on." He stepped inside, with Toby on his heels. Their shoes made no sound on the soft Persian rug that covered the entryway. Shaun was about to call for the doctor again, when something on the floor stopped him.

Shaun pointed at the shotgun lying on the rug.

"Is that blood on the barrel?" Toby mumbled.

"Okay," Shaun said. "New plan."

"I'm listening."

"Something has obviously happened here. Maybe a break-in. So let's drop the groceries, back on out, and go find Sheriff Rosco."

"Ah, dude," Toby said, his voice trembling. "I found him."

Shaun spun around. Toby was staring into the drawing room.

"But I don't think he's gonna be much help," Toby added.

Shaun stepped past Toby and peered into the still room. Lying on the floor, with blood staining his special black-and-yellow Founder's Day uniform, lay the motionless, portly body of Sheriff Rosco.

CHAPTER 3

DEATH IS FOREVER

Shaun was close to hyperventilating. He pulled out his inhaler and took a squirt. In a few moments he began to breathe normally, or as close to normal as he could get while staring at a dead body.

"Can I have a hit of that?" Toby asked.

Shaun handed it over, and Toby shot a quick pump into his lungs. "Thanks, man," Toby said, then handed it back.

"Anytime," Shaun mumbled, his eyes locked on the dead body just a few feet away. "Now what?"

Toby snapped his fingers, then reached into his pocket. "Call for help." Toby pulled out his cell phone.

"No reception out here," Shaun said.

Toby smacked his phone. "World's biggest network my butt."

"Land line," Shaun said, eyeing a phone resting on a table in the hallway.

Toby snatched up the receiver and dialed. He flashed a look of disappointment. "Does the Doc pay his bills?"

"Why?"

Toby put the receiver back in the cradle. "Cause the phone is dead."

"We could try the CB." Shaun pointed at the mic resting on the dead man's shoulder.

"Excellent," Toby said. "You go make the call. I'll cover you from here."

Shaun stared at him. "Cover me with what?"

"Ah." Toby smiled. "Warm, happy thoughts."

Shaun wrapped an arm around Toby's back and pushed him in the room.

"Fine," Toby said, stumbling forward. They both knelt on opposite sides of the body, and Toby whispered, "How do we know he's dead?"

Shaun looked at the Sheriff's round face. The last time he'd seen it, the Sheriff was scolding him for riding his bike on the sidewalk. As he checked the big man over, Shaun had no doubt that the Sheriff's scolding days were over. "Well," Shaun whispered. "He's not breathing, he looks pale, and his eyes are open and glassy. How much deader do you want him to be?"

Toby shrugged, then whispered, "That's dead enough, I guess."

"Why are we whispering?" Shaun asked.

"I don't know," Toby said. "Just seemed like the thing to do, you know, like when you're in church or a museum."

"Or when you find a dead body in a mad scientist's house."

"Exactly."

"Can we stop now?"

"Yeah," Toby said, pointing to the CB. "You know how to work that thing?"

"Why me?" Shaun asked.

"It was your idea."

Shaun slumped, then held up a fist. "Shoot for it?"

Toby sighed, nodded, and held out his fist. "Okay."

The boys said in unison, "Rock-paper-scissors-lizard-Spock, shoot," while pumping their fists.

Creating a thick V with his fingers, Toby threw a Spock.

Shaun shaped his hand to look like a reptile's mouth. "Lizard beats Spock, dude."

"I know." Toby reached for the CB. "Vulcans are supposed to be super intelligent. You'd think they could out smart a stupid lizard."

His hand hovered over the CB, clearly trying to figure out how to unhook it without touching blood. With a deep breath Toby snatched it up, then checked it over for crimson splashes. Satisfied, he brought

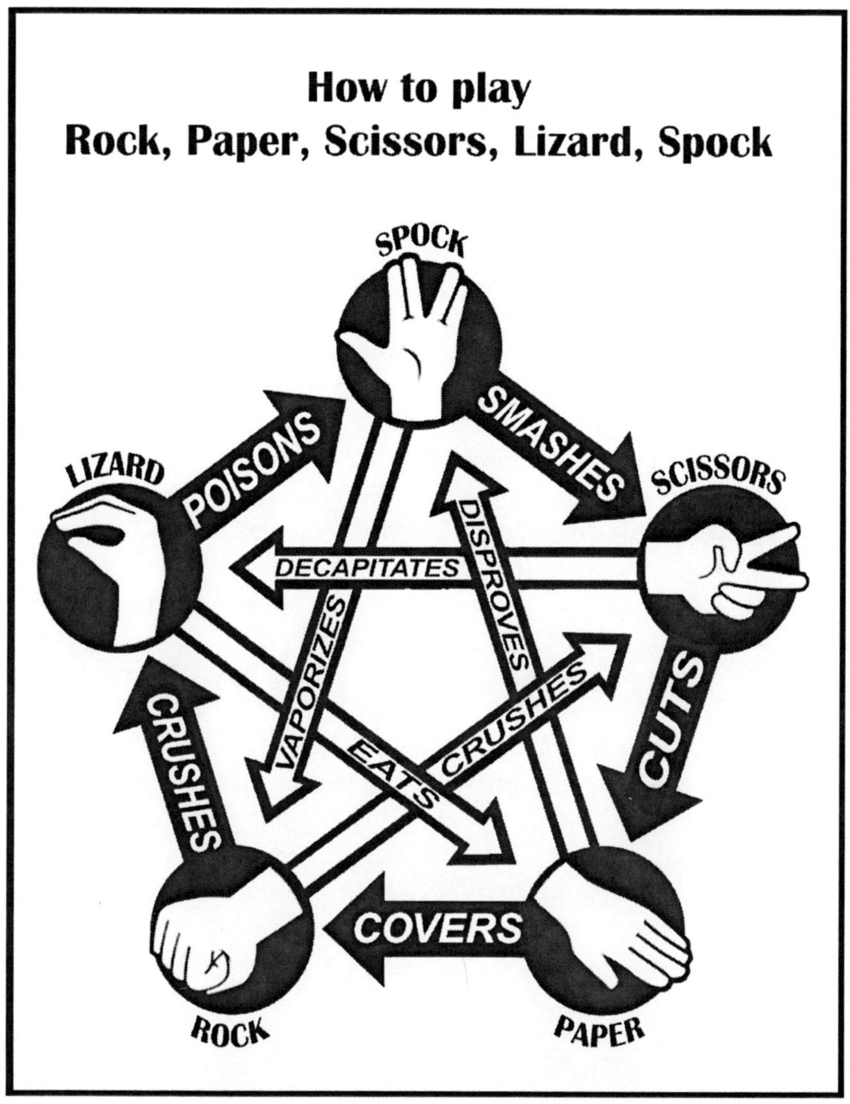

it to his lips, and pressed the call button. "Ah, hello," he began. "Mayday, mayday. S.O.S. Hello."

Shaun smacked his lips. "Dude, we're not shipwrecked."

Toby lowered the CB. "Well, excuse me. It's my first time finding a dead body."

Shaun's heart skipped a beat as he glimpsed a flesh-colored lump on the other side of the room. "Correction. Two dead bodies."

Toby followed Shaun's gaze to where a woman lay sprawled

across the couch like someone's dirty laundry. Her limbs dangled above the carpet, and blood dripped into her blond hair, from which sprouted black-and-yellow bee antennas.

Toby shot to his feet. "Okay, I'm outta here. Two dead bodies in one room is my limit."

"Right there with you, man," Shaun said and started moving toward the door. But before either of them could get out of the room, a horrific buzzing filled the entryway. They both stopped and stared at the open front door, neither of them moving as the buzzing got louder. Shaun's lungs tightened, and as he reached for his inhaler a monstrous bee the size of a Chihuahua flew in through the open door. It hovered in the entryway, turning, scanning. Four wings, each larger than playing cards, flapped in a blur of motion, keeping the six-legged creature aloft. Its long, sleek abdomen comprised more than half its body length, making it look more wasp-like than bee. But as its apple-sized head swiveled to look at them with black compound eyes, and wiry hair stood up along its thorax, Shaun could see it was definitely a bee.

Shaun's lungs contracted, but before the chest pain started, he felt Toby's hand on his shirt. His friend yanked him to the floor as the bee attacked. The giant insect zipped overhead, stinger out and ready for business. Speed and momentum carried the bee through an open window, then the creature stopped, turned around and charged again.

Shaun rolled one way and Toby the other. Shaun scurried over Sheriff Rosco's body and then pushed himself up by a plush reading chair. The hideous bee changed directions and went after Toby. Toby screamed. Shaun felt helpless as Toby raised his hands to fend off the dagger-like stinger.

Without thinking, Shaun snatched a pillow from the chair and chucked it like a Chinese throwing star. The pillow, twice the size of the bee, hit the insect dead on. The pillow crashed into a table lamp then hit the wall. When it came to rest on the floor, Shaun saw a stinger pierce the corduroy fabric in the pillow.

Toby jumped up and dashed over to him. "Nice shot, dude. Very James Bond."

Shaun pulled out his inhaler and took a hit. On an average day Shaun took a shot once or maybe twice a day. At this pace his inhaler would be bone-dry within the hour.

The pillow rolled over with a soft thump, and the bee frantically tried to extract its stinger. It came out with a puff of feathers, and the bee fumbled across the floor.

"Hey," Toby said. "It's not dying. It still has its stinger."

"What?" Shaun said, trying to breathe.

"Normally, bees can only sting once, then they die."

The bee rose off the floor, buzzing angrily.

"Newsflash," Shaun said. "That bee isn't normal."

The insect turned its gruesome face toward Shaun and Toby, and its buzzing became a roar that Shaun could feel in his chest.

"Wow, he's really mad," Toby said.

The flying beast charged them again.

Shaun and Toby took off running. They sprinted through open rooms, bumping into each other, as they took turns to glance back. Every time Shaun looked over his shoulder, the buzzing got closer. It sounded as if the thing was close enough to land on his head, but just before it did Toby screamed, "Duck!"

Turning forward, Shaun saw something white and stringy spanning the entryway to the kitchen. Toby slipped under it like a runner sliding home, and Shaun skidded down right behind him. They tumbled into the kitchen slamming into counters and chairs.

Shaun jumped up immediately expecting to fight for his life. He brought up his fists and scanned the room. No bee. He looked back into the hallway and found the thing, struggling, squirming — stuck in the enormous spider web spun across the kitchen entryway. The boys had slid under it, but the giant bee hadn't been so lucky. Its wings were held tight by thick strands of silk, and it seemed to become more entangled as it fought to break free.

Something buzzed over Shaun's head, and he instinctively ducked. Toby got to his feet and the two boys stood mesmerized, watching Dr. Romero's eight-legged Bumblebeeder fly to its web and land next to the monster bee. The Bumblebeeder seized the giant insect around the head in its horrific tarantella-like mandibles. The bee tried to sting its attacker, but the Bumblebeeder moved out of the way and thrust black paralyzing fangs deep into the bee's thorax. The bee convulsed, then slumped. Immediately the Bumblebeeder began spinning its prize into a preserving cocoon of silk.

"Dude," Toby said, panting. "That could possibly be the sickest thing I've ever seen."

"Sick like cool, or sick like super gross?"

Toby shook his head. "I haven't decided yet."

Shaun put a hand on his chest. His heart pounded so hard he could feel it in his temples. "Do you know what a stroke feels like?"

Before Toby answered, something burst from the pantry. Shaun spun around, and the first thing he saw was the meat cleaver, its stainless steel blade glinting in the kitchen light.

Shaun and Toby screamed in unison, as the cleaver loomed overhead.

The man holding it stopped in the middle of the kitchen and joined their panicked screams. The three stood motionless, all staring at one another, screaming. Suddenly the man with the cleaver winced in pain, clutched at his bloody shoulder, then dropped to his knees.

He fell forward with a loud plop, and the cleaver skidded across the linoleum.

Toby leaned against a counter, hand over his heart, and met Shaun's gaze. "Dude, I don't care how much you offer to pay me, I am *NOT* going on any more of your deliveries."

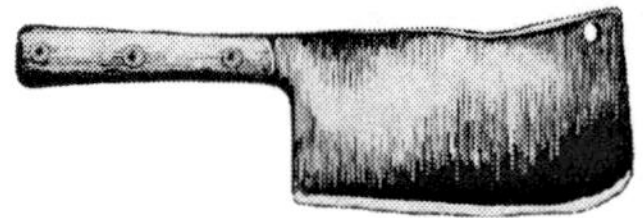

CHAPTER 4
THE MAN WITH THE RED TATTOO

"Dr. Romero!" Shaun rolled the man over on the kitchen floor. The man's thick, black-framed glasses sat askew on his long, thin nose. Looking as if it hadn't been combed in a decade, his ghost-white hair was disobedient in all directions. Blood spotted his oversized lab coat and sticking out of his chest like a mast on a ship was a huge syringe. Its contents had already been injected.

"Is he dead?' Toby asked.

Shaun shook his head. "No idea."

Dr. Romero's eyes popped open and he sat up fast like someone waking from a nightmare. Toby and Shaun fell to the floor and slid backward in case the doctor came at them again.

"Shaun," the doctor said with a slight European accent. "What in the devil are you doing here, my boy?"

I've been asking myself the same question. "I brought your groceries."

"Oh, right, groceries." He looked around. "What am I doing on the floor?'

"You passed out," Shaun said.

"After you attacked us with this," Toby added, holding up the cleaver.

The doctor's eyes suddenly went wide and his mouth fell open as if he had remembered something. "Have you seen any *Apis mellifera gigantus*?"

Shaun furrowed his brow. "*Apis melli*—what?"

"Large bees," Dr. Romero said.

"Like that?" Toby pointed to the web where the Bumblebeeder was putting the finishing touches on a cocoon.

"Oh, dear," Dr. Romero said. "So they made it out of the lab."

"What," Shaun said. "What made it out of the lab?"

"Have you seen Sheriff Rosco or anyone from animal control?" Dr. Romero asked.

Shaun and Toby shot each other uncomfortable glances, both recalling the bloody scene at the other end of the house. Shaun nodded. "We've seen them, Doc."

"Excellent," Dr. Romero said. "We may be able to salvage this situation. Help me up boys." The doctor held out his arms and Toby and Shaun each took one, and helped him up. Shaun had to step back so he didn't get poked in the eye by the syringe protruding from the doctor's chest.

"Now, then," Dr. Romero said. "Where are they?"

"There're in the front room," Toby said. "Dead."

"Dead?" Dr. Romero stood a little straighter, raised an eyebrow. "How dead?"

"How dead?" Shaun repeated. "Like, all the way. Do not hit reset. Do not pass go. Dead-dead."

"Show me," Dr. Romero said as he headed for the Bumblebeeder's web. He ducked under the massive strands of silk as if it were something he did everyday. He shouted over his shoulder. "Come along boys. It won't bother you."

Toby smirked. "Yeah right, said the crazy man in the bloody lab coat, with a needle in his chest."

Dr. Romero continued down the hall, and since the doctor was the only one who might know what was going on, Shaun felt compelled to follow. "Come on, Toby."

When he ducked under the Bumblebeeder's silky net of spidery-death, Shaun held his breath and closed his eyes. He had no idea why he held his breath, but he closed his eyes because, if an eight-legged Creature Feature monster was about to drop down on him, he had no interest in watching it happen.

Toby joined him on the other side. They plodded down the hall.

Dr. Romero was already out of sight, but they found him in the front room, hands on the side of his face looking like that *Home Alone* kid.

"Oh, my, they *are* dead," Dr. Romero said. "I just know this will come out of my funding."

As Shaun neared, the doctor looked down at him, then began patting his pockets. "Ah, boys, when you found me did you see a syringe nearby?"

Toby reached up, plucked the syringe out of the doctor's chest, then held it up for him to see. "Did it look like this?"

Shaun was surprised at Toby and shot him a look. "Dude?"

Dr. Romero glanced down at his chest, then to the syringe. "Thank you my boy." He took it from Toby's hand and examined it. "That's not good. I've injected myself with the entire supply." The doctor then began mumbling, as if thinking aloud.

"Well, that explains why I'm lucid." He looked down at his lab coat and the dime-sized hole outlined in crimson. "The blood loss is the reason for the light-headedness and the lapse in consciousness. And the large dose of the antidote explains the momentary psychotic behavior." He opened his shirt and revealed a large half dollar-sized area of discolored skin.

At first Shaun thought it was a red tattoo, some type of Japanese symbol, but then he realized it was the wound left by the syringe.

"That's not pretty," Toby said.

"Doctor," Shaun said. "What's going on?"

Shaun's words seem to snap Dr. Romero back to attention, but he ignored the question. "Boys, you need to help me tie them down."

"Tie who down?" Toby said.

Dr. Romero stepped into the drawing room, heading straight for the nearest body. "Sheriff Rosco and this poor woman."

Shaun didn't understand. "Why do we need to tie the bodies down? They're dead."

Dr. Romero bent over and picked up the sheriff's wrists. "Boys, grab his legs. There's not much time. I'll explain on the way."

Shaun and Toby exchanged confused looks then stepped over to the dead man's feet. Shaun grunted as they lifted.

"Why do we get the heavy end?" Toby said.

Shaun watched the three-hundred-pound man jiggle. "I don't think there is a light end, dude."

"Where to, Doc?" Toby said.

Dr. Romero moved first, sidestepping carefully. "This way, into the laboratory. I have a large specimen table. We'll strap him down there."

The boys huffed and puffed as the sheriff's dead butt slid along the floor.

Dr. Romero seemed in good shape, despite his age and the hole in his shoulder. His voice remained even as he spoke. "Three months ago, the military…uh, I mean a client, requested that I try to reproduce a top secret trioxin-based compound. They had been unable to synthesize the substance themselves and asked me to find a natural means of replication."

"What does this…secret compound stuff…do?" Shaun spoke through clenched teeth.

"It has the ability to regenerate dead or dying cells," Dr. Romero said. "Its applications in the medical field, healing wounds and such, would revolutionize modern medicine."

"But they can't make…enough?" Toby said.

"Correct." Dr. Romero turned, stepping backward into a hallway. "The substance's close chemical makeup to that of bee venom gave me the idea to attempt to create an insect that could manufacture the compound and deliver it through their stingers."

"Did the substance make the bees giant size?" Shaun asked.

"No. This way, boys," Dr. Romero said, shuffling into the laboratory. "Their unusual size was by design. In order to reproduce the compound in vast quantities, I increased their size with various growth hormones of my own mixing."

"The bigger the bug, the more stuff it can make," Shaun said. "But, besides their size they still don't look like normal bees."

"Good observation, Shaun. I spliced the DNA of several different species, even took some parasitic qualities from the *Apocephalus borealis.* But the largest contribution comes from the vespid wasp. This gave my new breed a reusable stinger. Not absolutely reusable, but one able to inject venom three to five times before its stinger dislodges and the bee dies. It's the only fail-safe I was able to come up with, in the event that…well, what has happened, happens. O'kay, right here boys."

The large steel table stood about as high as a kitchen counter. "We can't lift him that high," Shaun said.

"Give it a go," Dr. Romero said. "You're stronger than you

know."

The doctor was right. It took some doing but they got the obese black-and-yellow clad Sheriff Rosco up onto the table. Toby leaned forward and put both hands on his knees, then said, "So you built in a fail-safe in case these things ever get out."

Dr. Romero nodded. "The wasp DNA makes them highly territorial and aggressive."

"We noticed," Shaun said, gazing around the lab. It was different from the last time he'd been here. Equipment had been upended, glass specimen aquariums smashed, and windows broken outward.

"They will attack other insects without provocation, and the color combination of black and yellow sends them into a hostile frenzy."

Toby straightened up. "So how did they get out?"

Dr. Romero turned around and pointed at the massive, wall-size glass panel that took up a third of the lab. Every time Shaun had toured this room, a tombstone-colored curtain had been drawn over it. But now, the curtain lay strewn across the floor, and he could see giant honeycombs on the other side of the glass. The hexagonal openings in the wax cells were at least ten times normal size.

"I was giving them their daily dose of growth hormone," Romero said, looking disappointed with himself. "I had done it so many times. Perhaps I became complacent, but one of them escaped my notice in the isolation area. It shot straight at me, stung my shoulder, and I must have inadvertently released the containment latch."

Shaun looked up at the huge, empty cage. "How many were in there, Doc?"

"There were six hundred and sixty-seven inside."

"Oh man," Toby said. "We have to tell someone. The Army, the Navy, Animal Planet, somebody!"

"I tried," Dr, Romero said. "Not thinking too clearly I immediately called Sheriff Rosco. He said he'd bring someone from Animal Control. But after I hung up I remembered there was an emergency number."

"What emergency number?" Shaun said.

"The secret compound came in a container with a number on it, and in case of contamination, I'm supposed to call and report it." Dr. Romero pointed at a rusty steel barrel with capital letters stenciled in yellow on the side.

Shaun stepped forward to read it.

PROPERTY
DEPARTMENT OF ARMY
IN CASE OF EMERGENCY
CALL -311-555-8674

"What happened when you called?" Toby said.

"They asked me where I obtained the substance, then asked if I'd been infected. I told them I had, but I planned to use the antitoxin I had created, which should counter the effects. I was put on hold for what seemed like a few minutes, then the line went dead. I tried calling back, but I couldn't get a dial tone, after that."

"That's fascinating and all," Shaun said, "but you still haven't explained why we need to tie the Sheriff's dead body down."

"Oh, my," Dr. Romero said with a start. "I forgot. Will you grab all the surgical tape you can out of that drawer?"

Toby spun on a heel, opened a steel drawer, and started pulling out rolls of thick white tape. Dr. Romero snatched several rolls and handed some to Shaun. "Wrap his legs, quickly."

All three went to work. Shaun started at the sheriff's ankles, then handed the tape under the table to Toby, who brought it over the top.

"It's the substance," Dr, Romero said. "A single sting contains a mutated version of the substance. A thousand times a normal dose and loaded with insect DNA, death occurs in just a few minutes."

"But you're alive," Shaun said, handing the roll under the table to Toby.

"That's because I was able to get to my antitoxin in time—the syringe you found. The enormous amount of substance and antidote in my body made me delusional for a while, but I think I'm all right now."

Don't bet on it, Shaun thought.

"Sheriff Rosco and that poor woman out front received a sting that killed them, but if I am correct, cellular regeneration will occur on a massive scale."

Shaun finished taping the legs and stepped back. "How massive?"

Dr. Romero wrapped tape around the sheriff's chest. "Completely, resulting in total re-animation."

Toby stepped away from the table. "Re-what?!"

"Reanimation," Shaun said. "You mean like zombies?!"

Dr. Romero didn't answer. He just handed them each more tape and said, "Work faster, please."

They snatched the tape and worked five times faster than before. All Shaun could hear was tape being pulled from the spools and his heart pounding like a sledge hammer.

When more than half of the sheriff's body looked like an Egyptian mummy, the three stood back, breathing heavy. Shaun's lungs ached. He reached in his pocket and took a hit from his inhaler. After a deep calming breath, he gazed at the still body of Sheriff Rosco. "If he wakes up this will officially be my least favorite day. Ever."

Toby nodded. "True story, man."

"Come on boys," Dr. Romero said. "We've got one more."

Reluctantly, they followed the doctor out of the lab. As they retraced their steps back to the front of the house, Shaun wondered at exactly what point in the day things took a turn for the weird. He had started it off eating Corn Flakes and arguing with his mom about what to wear. But by mid-afternoon he and his best friend Toby were helping Doctor Bee'nstein carry dead bodies through his creepy old house. *How does this freaking happen?*

Then something his mom had said stuck out in his mind. She was urging him to think about honoring the town's traditions when she said, "Absolutely everyone will be in costume today." The realization of what this meant felt like a wasp sting to the brain.

"Ah guys," Shaun said.

The doctor and Toby stopped in the entryway to the drawing room and turned to face him. "What is it, Shaun," Dr. Romero said. "We haven't much time."

Shaun held up a finger. "This will just take a sec. On the way here, Toby and I heard lots of buzzing overhead while we were in the grove about a mile from your house. Seemed like it was heading toward town."

Toby shrugged. "We don't know which way they were going. They could have been heading out to sea for all we—"

"Dude," Shaun said. "Do the frickin' math. If you minus the one the Bumblebeeder-thing wrapped up for dinner, that means there are six hundred and sixty-six giant bees—"

"*Apis mellifera gigantus*," Dr. Romero corrected.

"Whatever," Shaun snapped. "There are six hundred and sixty-six angry, territorial, multiple-stinging, mutant bees that are wired to attack anything black and yellow heading straight for a town where everyone is dressed in bumblebee costumes?"

"Oh, dear," Dr. Romero said, his face turning white. "It's Founder's Day, isn't it?"

"Yeah," Shaun said. "Same day every year, for like the last hundred years."

"This is bad." The doctor slumped into a chair. "Very bad indeed."

"Ah, Doc," Toby said, pointing. "I think things are about to get worse."

"How could it possibly get worse?" Shaun said and looked where Toby was pointing. As Shaun stared at the empty couch, the seat cushions stained red, it took a second to sink in. But only a second. "Oh, yeah," he said. "It's worse."

"Where did…" Toby said, his voice shaky. "…the dead animal control lady go?"

CHAPTER

5

THE FACTS OF DEATH

It's unsettling to see adults frightened, and as Shaun looked up at Dr. Romero he definitely felt unsettled.

The doctor ran his long fingers through his unruly hair, eyes wide, lower lip quivering. "That poor woman."

"Ah, doc," Shaun said.

The doctor blinked hard a few times, his fluffy white eyebrows bouncing.

Shaun gazed at the front door standing wide open. "Is that woman going to be all right?"

Dr. Romero shook his head slightly. "I don't know. Maybe."

"Well, is she dead or not?" Toby said.

"She most likely is neither dead nor alive." Dr. Romero removed his glasses and wiped his forehead. "She is…in between."

Shaun had no idea what that meant, but before he could ask, Dr. Romero turned to face them. "Boys, I need your help. The way I see it, there are two problems to address."

"Only two?" Toby said.

"One, we need to find that woman. If I can administer the antitoxin, perhaps she has a chance."

Toby turned to Shaun. "Did he say we?"

"And second, we need to warn the town. If Shaun is right, there is a chance that the *Apis mellifera gigantus* will target Honeywell Springs."

Shaun leaned toward Toby. "Yeah, he definitely said we."

"So, boys..." Dr. Romero leaned forward and placed a hand on each of their shoulders. "I need you to do one of two things. Option one, go outside and search for the animal control woman while I begin formulating some new antitoxin."

Helping the doctor carry a dead body from one end of the house to the other was one thing, but hunting for a reanimated corpse that was walking around? No way!

"What's option two?" Shaun asked.

"With the phones out, we need to get word to town. The unnatural size of *Apis mellifera gigantus* makes them clumsy and slow, especially in the air. I think you two could ride your bikes back to town and easily beat them there. Find the mayor and tell him what is going on. Instruct him to get everyone inside before it's too late."

Jeez. Hunt for a zombie around Dr. Romero's house, or ride bikes back to town with six hundred and sixty-six monster mutant bees flying overhead. Was it Shaun's imagination, or was this day getting worse?

Toby smiled and took Shaun by the elbow. "Excuse us a second, Doc. Just want to have a private chat with my friend here."

"Be quick about it. Time is of the essence." Dr. Romero spun around. "I'll be in the lab. Let me know what you decide."

When the doctor was well out of earshot, Toby dropped the smile like a hundred-pound barbell. "I have a third option."

"Thank God," Shaun said. "I'm all ears."

"We tell Doctor Freakshow to sit and spin, and you and I go find someplace to hide until this all blows over."

"Excellent," Shaun agreed. "Where do you want to hide?"

"Well, not around here with the *Dawn of the Dead* lady walking around, waiting to eat our brains!"

"If she is after brains, I'm sure you'll be safe," Shaun said.

"Ha, ha," Toby said. "You know of any good hiding places?"

Shaun was about to make a suggestion, but something didn't feel right. The idea of hiding when everybody they knew—family, friends, even the bullies and crabby Mr. Hooper—were all in danger didn't sit well. He reached in his pocket and pulled out his inhaler. "Maybe..." he said. "Maybe we should go to town."

"No way, dude," Toby said. "Getting killed by a swarm of giant mutant bees is way down on my to-do list."

"Hey, I don't want to die, either," Shaun said. "But running away and hiding when everyone we know is in danger doesn't feel very James Bond-like. Did 007 run away when Dr. No threaten to disrupt the Project Mercury space launch with an atomic-powered radio beam?"

"Well, no."

"Did Bond bail out on Pussy Galore after decompressing the plane and blowing Goldfinger out a window?"

"Of course not," Toby said.

"Did he stay hidden when M needed him after MI-6 headquarters got blown up?"

"But dude, James Bond is fiction, and even if he wasn't, he never faced down giant killer bees or the walking dead."

"And neither are we," Shaun said, putting a hand on Toby's shoulder. "Look, all I'm saying is, we go in fast, find the mayor, tell him what's going on, and we come out heroes."

"Heroes?" Toby smirked. "People call me geezer pants, and you haven't gone ten minutes today without a hit from that thing." Toby jabbed a finger at Shaun's inhaler. "The dynamic duo we are *soooo* not."

Shaun looked at his inhaler. His hand was shaking and he could feel his lungs growing tight. He took a small squirt, followed by a deep breath.

"Face it, man," Toby said. "We're not the hero types."

"Maybe today we are." Shaun stuck the inhaler back in his pocket. "C'mon man, what do you say? It's 007 time."

Toby didn't answer. His lips tightened and Shaun could tell his friend was seriously considering the idea. But before Toby could make up his mind, a scurrying motion caught their attention. The two boys gazed down the long corridor to the kitchen and saw the horrific Bumblebeeder crawl onto the ceiling, mandibles clicking. It hissed at them like a feral cat.

They both took a retreating step toward the front door. "The doctor said it wouldn't hurt us, remember?" Shaun said.

Toby gulped. "Is that the same doctor that just unleashed a swarm of killer BeeZillas on the world?"

"Good point," Shaun said as they both took another backward

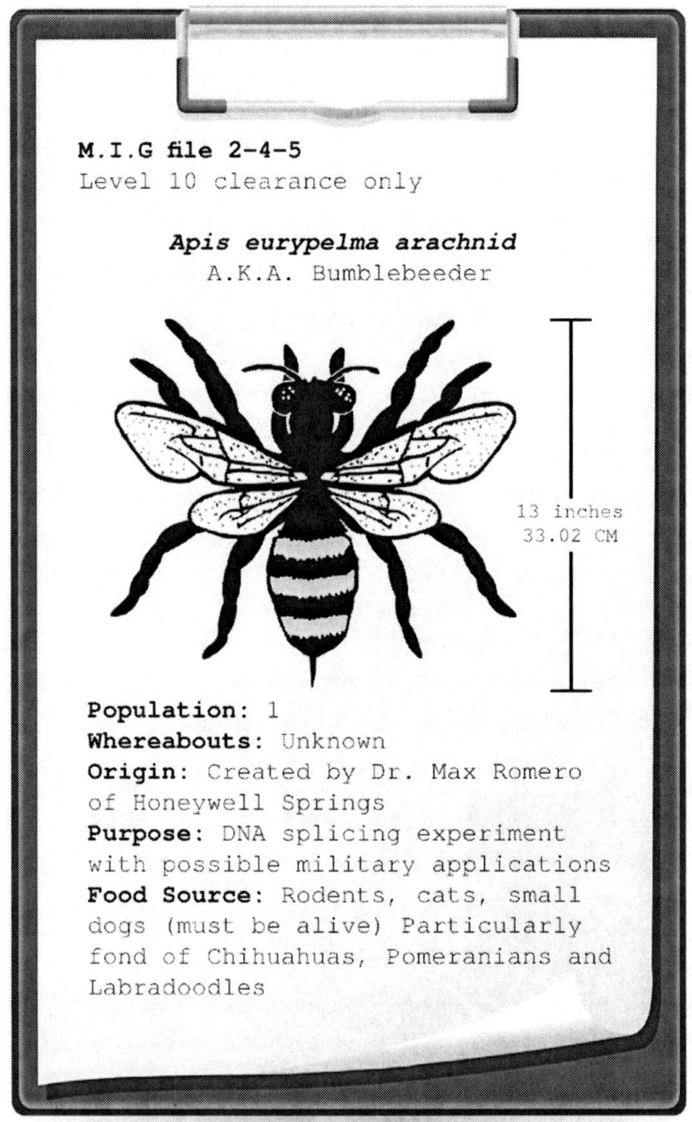

step. "Ready to go be heroes?"

"I can't wait to be a hero," Toby said, as they both turned and bolted through the entryway.

"We'll warn the town, Doc," Shaun said as they ran out the front door, down the steps and jumped on their bikes. As they started to roll down the long dirt driveway, Shaun tossed out the rest of the groceries, like a hot air balloon dropping sand bags.

Toby shouted over his shoulder. "You want to go the way we came? It's longer."

Shaun considered for a moment. If those things were still in the sky, there were more places to hide along the route they had traveled earlier. The other way, the most direct route to Honeywell Springs and Main Street, would take them through open fields. He didn't like the idea of getting caught in the open with six hundred and sixty-six multiple-stinging bees overhead. In fact, it was his worst nightmare.

"Yeah," Shaun yelled. "Back to the golf course."

They zipped through the overhanging groove with speed that shook their handlebars so hard Shaun thought he'd lose control. He managed to keep from crashing and they only slowed on the curves, their tires sliding in the loose gravel.

Soon they were cutting back across the golf course, Shaun breathing so hard he felt on the verge of puking. He was thankful that Toby stopped in the middle of the eleventh green.

Toby seemed fixated on a speck of blue over by the golf cart rental shack. "Hey, is that Sam's motorcycle?"

Shaun leaned forward on his handlebars, feeling nauseated. "I don't know. What if it is?"

"I thought she was heading back to town. She should be there by now."

"And?"

"Why would she leave her bike?"

"Who cares!" Shaun said. "Maybe she went to go get her dad, so they could come back and pick it up with his truck."

Toby shook his head. "Then she'd get busted for riding a motorcycle on the golf course."

That did make sense. "Okay, so what's your theory, genius?"

Toby shrugged. "I don't know. Maybe she is in trouble."

"Yeah," Shaun said. "Join the club."

"Let's just go check, real quick." Toby was about to start peddling.

Shaun reached over and grabbed the sleeve of Toby's black-and-yellow sweater. "Dude, just a little while ago you wanted us to find a place and hide. Now you want to go help someone who dumped a cherry slushy on your head last summer?"

Toby spun around to face Shaun. "Look, we're on a mission to warn the town, and Sam is part of the town." Toby wrenched his sleeve away and started rolling toward the golf cart shack.

"Yeah, she's the part of the town that calls you pansy-pants." Shaun watched Toby go. "And when did this become a mission, exactly?"

Shaun sat by himself for a minute. *Does Toby have a little thing for Sam?* He funneled his hands around his mouth and yelled, "Is this because you think she's cute?"

Toby ignored him and biked down the fairway.

Reluctantly, Shaun peddled after Toby. *This is a waste of time.* But it wouldn't be the first colossal waste of time they'd spent chasing a girl that Toby had a crush on. Last Christmas break, Shaun helped Toby learn some Korean so he could speak to a cute exchange student who was attending Honeywell Springs Middle School for the semester. They spent three weeks memorizing phrases, and even a few jokes, only to learn that Chinese exchange students don't speak a whole lot of Korean.

By the time Shaun reached the golf cart shack, Toby was off his bike and calling out Sam's name. "Hey, Sam. Sam, are you here? Sam!"

"We're wasting time, dude," Shaun said.

Toby headed toward the large aluminum-sided shack. Its barn-sized double doors that led into the repair area stood wide open.

Shaun was about to follow, when he heard a loud hiss, like air escaping a tire. At least that's what it sounded like over Toby's shouting. As Shaun set his bike down next to Toby's, the hissing became a shushing, followed by, "Hey, dork, will you tell geezer-pants to shut up?"

Shaun looked up into a spruce tree to find Sam, crouching like a frightened squirrel, on a high branch.

"Sam?" Shaun made no effort to be quiet. "What're you doing?"

"Shut up," Sam said, no longer whispering. Her eyes darted over to the golf shack. "Oh, man, its back."

Shaun followed her gaze. "What's back?" He slapped a hand over his mouth as one of Dr. Romero's mutant bees moved across the top of the shack, its tarsal claws clicking on the metal roof. In its long feelers it pinched what was left of a small bird, its black-and-yellow feathers speckled with blood and its head dragging from an exposed spine.

Shaun stepped behind the tree and looked for Toby. His friend had moved into the shack, and Shaun could hear him rummaging around like someone going through a garbage can for recyclables.

Jeez, could he make any more noise?

A second later Toby strolled out with a wrench and screwdriver in his hands. "She must have come here to fix her…"

Waving his arms wildly, Shaun got Toby's attention.

Toby smiled as if he'd just heard a lame joke. "Dude, are you trying to fly or what?"

"Look out!" Shaun shouted as the bee dropped its feathery lunch and took to the air.

Toby turned around and looked up as the bee dived. The flying terror closed the distance fast, not at all slow like Dr. Romero asserted. Toby dropped the tools and ducked back into the shack. Shaun heard a crash. The bee darted inside with a horrific buzz.

Shaun ran to help his friend. Scooping up the wrench and holding it like a sword, he peered inside the shack. Shaun spied Toby crawling backward on the cement floor, pausing only to hurl something at the black-and-yellow monster in front of him.

"Bad bee!" Toby screamed. "Go away! I'm totally not worth stinging."

The bee hovered over Toby, as if it was waiting for an open shot. It clearly didn't detect Shaun as he took aim and chucked the wrench. It twirled in the air like a boomerang, but only grazed the bee's long black legs. The tool hit the back wall with a pounding rattle. Tools and maintenance equipped hanging on the wall crashed to the floor.

The noise disoriented the bee for a moment, enough time for Toby to regain his feet. He ran for the shack's entrance, but the bee circled and then zipped to cut off his escape route. The bee buzzed right by Shaun's head.

Shaun ducked low and then darted into the shack. Toby, realizing he was cut off, skidded to a stop and began backing up, slowly, his hands out in defense.

Shaun looked for something to throw. From a box of what looked like electric motor parts he pulled out something metal and greasy the size of a softball. He tried to take aim, but Toby was in his line of fire.

"Toby, duck!" Shaun screamed.

Obediently, Toby dropped like a stone, and Shaun hurled the greasy motor part. Because it was heavy, Shaun put everything he had into the pitch, which caused the hunk of metal to sail clear over the bee and out of the shack, disappearing in the sunlight. There was a soft thud, immediately followed by a loud cry.

Outside, Sam crumbled to the cement driveway her hands clasped over one knee. "You idiot!" Apparently Sam had descended from the tree and was making her escape when Shaun's bad aim took her down.

"Sorry," Shaun yelled.

Jumping to his feet, Toby found himself nose to nose with the bee. He screamed, then punched the bee square in its bug-eyed face. Stunned, the bee spiraled toward the ground.

Shaun wasted no time. He picked up an empty wooden crate, rushed at the bee and slapped the crate over the insect, pushing it to the ground. Trapped inside, the bee buzzed angrily.

Shaun stood up, and backed over to Toby.

Toby slapped a hand on Shaun's shoulder. "Dude, quick thinking. I never would've thought of that."

Shaun tried to take a breath but it was difficult. He bent forward with his hands on his knees, but managed a smile. "How about you, man. You punched it, all Chuck Norris and everything."

Toby chuckled. "Yeah, I don't know what came over me."

Shaun stood up and managed a deep breath. "I thought we were dead meat."

"Hey, did you find Sam?" Toby said.

"Yeah, but…" His words trailed off as they watched the crate slowly rise into the air. It wobbled in front of them as if pulled up by fishing line.

"You have got to be *fricking* kidding me," Toby said, clutching Shaun's shoulder.

The crate tilted to the side, its opening sliding toward the top. A moment later the crate bounced to the cement floor, leaving the bee hanging in the air. It whirled around to face the boys.

"You think it's mad?" Shaun said, whimpering.

"Furious," Toby said, then pointed at Shaun. "Ah, he did it."

"Dude!"

"Sorry, bro. I'm panicking."

"Me too."

It was hard to tell, but the bee seemed to be switching its attention between Shaun and Toby, like someone watching a tennis match.

"I think it's dizzy or something," Toby said.

"Yeah," Shaun said. "Or it can't decide which one of us to kill first."

Toby pointed at Shaun again.

"Dude!" Shaun said.

Toby dropped his finger. "Sorry, man. Still panicking."

"It's okay."

"All right," Toby said. "I got a plan. Let's back up, real slow."

They both took careful steps back, neither of them taking their eyes off the monstrous bee. It flew forward, matching each of Shaun and Toby's retreating steps. After a few feet, Shaun felt the back wall of the shed, cold and solid behind him. The bee buzzed. "Okay, I'm ready to hear the next part of this plan of yours."

"Uh," Toby stammered. "In my plan there's not a wall right here."

Shaun rolled his eyes. "Ahhh, man."

"Well, I haven't heard you make any suggestions."

The bee seemed to suddenly focus on Toby, antennas pointing forward, a hideous proboscis flicking out from between its feelers.

"Okay," Shaun said. "Plan B."

"Which is?" Toby asked.

The bee brought its stinger around and charged.

"Move!" Shaun screamed.

Toby rolled left and Shaun rolled right. There was a loud metal thump as the bee's stinger hit the aluminum wall between them. Shaun spun around and saw the bee struggling to pull its stinger from the wall, which had penetrated the aluminum like a railroad spike. Shaun's eyes widened as the stinger started to come free.

"Get out of the way!" Sam shrieked. Driving a golf cart, she plowed over their bikes and into the shack. Toby grabbed Shaun by the collar and yanked him back as Sam crashed the cart headlong into the back wall—and the bee.

The sound of the wrench hitting the aluminum wall was nothing compared to the explosion of the crashing golf cart. The tiny building thundered with an echoing, chaotic racket that took several moments to fade. As it did, dust sparkled in the sunlight bouncing off the ivory-colored golf cart. Sam lay slumped over the steering wheel. She sat up with effort, then winced and grabbed her right leg.

Shaun pushed himself off the floor, but Toby knocked him back down as he rushed by to get to the golf cart.

Toby put a hand on Sam's shoulder. "Are you all right?"

Sam slapped his hand away. "Don't touch me, dweeb."

Toby held up his hands apologetically. "Sorry."

Still holding her leg, Sam narrowed her eyes at Toby. "Are you the idiot that hit me with that, whatever it was?"

"Huh?"

Shaun raised his hand as he got to his feet. "I'm the idiot."

Sam turned her gaze on Shaun. "Nice shot. What were trying to do, kill me?"

"To be fair, I wasn't aiming for you."

"Oh, well, that makes my busted knee feel much better."

Shaun was about to tell her where she could stick her knee, when a sickly buzzing rattled from the front of the golf cart.

Toby and Shaun cautiously stepped over to the front of the cart. Crushed between the fiberglass hood and the shack's wall was what was left of the bee. Alien-like green ooze splattered the aluminum and dripped from mangled wings. Broken legs were twisted outward like crazy straws, and its head listed off its thorax, hanging by horrific strands of insect gore.

"Man," Toby said. "Those things are harder to kill than Jason Voorhees."

"Who?" Shaun asked.

"Horror guy. Never mind." Toby leaned forward, and the bee's head swiveled. "What should we do?"

"What do you mean?" Shaun asked.

Toby pointed at it. "It's suffering."

"Good," Sam said. "That makes two of us." She tried to lift her leg, bracing it with her hand.

"No, I mean we should put it out of its misery," Toby said. "Y'know, hit it with something big and heavy."

Shaun pointed to the golf cart. "Sam just did that."

"Dude…" Toby said.

"Fine," Shaun huffed. He looked around and saw a huge rubber mallet a few feet away. He snatched it up and thrust it out to Toby. "Knock yourself out."

"Uh, you get this one, I'll get the next one," Toby said, moving out of the way.

The bee's buzzing grew louder.

"Will you idiots just kill it already?" Sam barked.

Shaun rolled his eyes and stepped around to the front of the cart. The bee tried to turn its crushed head to face him. Shaun took a deep breath as he looked into its dying compound eyes. The dream-like memory of bees swarming over his body began to sting his mind, as he brought the mallet up. He tightened his grip, closed his eyes, then brought the mallet down with a sickening splat. Shaun withdrew the mallet slowly, opened one eye, then the other. The bee wasn't buzzing anymore. Headless bees have little buzz.

Where its head used to be was now a slushy mixture of insect exoskeleton and bee brains.

"Oh, that's just buckets of icky," Toby said, stepping up behind Shaun. "Very *Texas Chainsaw Massacre*."

"Did you get it?" Sam said.

"He got it," Toby said. "That's two down and six hundred and sixty-*five* to go."

The image of hundreds of monster bees diving on Honeywell Springs filled Shaun's mind. "We're gonna need a few more mallets."

CHAPTER

6

DOUBLE OR DIE

"You pulverized our bikes," Shaun said as Sam limped from the shack.

"Sorry," Sam said, hobbling to a tree. "Maybe you'd like the giant bee back?"

Shaun sighed. "It would have taken, what, two seconds to go around the bikes."

Sam leaned against the tree trunk. "If I took the time to go around, that thing would have wiggled loose, and I'm sure one or both of you would be very dead right now."

"We were doing just fine," Shaun snapped.

"Dude," Toby said.

"Okay, maybe not fine," Shaun corrected. "But we were real close to coming up with a plan, one that wouldn't have involved crushing our bikes!"

Sam winced, clutched her knee and slid to the ground. "Okay, I broke your bike and you broke my leg. Let's call it even."

Man, Shaun thought. *This is like the broken pickle jar all over again.* He was about to lay into her some more, but saw the pain on her face as she lay on the grass. Instantly, he felt like a jerk. "Is it really broke?" He knelt beside her.

Sam shook her head. "Just took a double-whammy. After you beaned me, I smacked the same leg into the steering wheel when I hit the wall."

A black grease mark on Sam's knee marked the spot where she'd been hit, and the skin around it was beginning to swell.

"I'm sorry, Sam," Shaun said. "I really wasn't trying to hit you."

"I know, dweeb," Sam said softly. "Sorry about your bikes."

"It's not so much the bikes," Toby said. "It's just that we're sort of on a mission."

Sam raised an eyebrow. "What kind of mis—" Sam suddenly winced and grabbed her leg.

"Shaun," Toby said, "can you go check the golf shack for a first aid kit? I'm pretty sure the maintenance guy keeps one in there."

Shaun nodded and moved back to the shack. As he rummaged around he could hear Toby catching Sam up on what had happened back at Dr. Romero's house, monster bees, top secret compound, dead sheriff, the whole nine yards. By the time he returned with the kit, Sam's face was all scrunched up as if she were staring at a college level trigonometry exam.

Sam looked up at Shaun. "Please tell me he's joking."

Shaun knelt down. "I wish I could."

Toby wrapped Sam's knee with an ACE bandage, while she just sat quietly. Shaun figured she was processing. It was a lot to absorb in just a few minutes, but he knew they didn't have a few minutes. They needed to get back on track immediately.

He glanced over to the row of golf carts, resting on the other side of the driveway. "Hey, Toby. Do you think one of those carts has enough juice to get us to town?"

"Yeah, of course they do. There and back a couple times, probably."

"Okay." Shaun stood. "That solves the transportation problem."

"I'll drive," Sam said, thrusting her hands out to them for assistance.

The boys each took a hand and helped Sam to her feet. "You don't have to go," Shaun said.

"Yes I do," Sam said. "So far today, I've ripped up the town's golf course on my motorcycle, broken into the golf shack, and was about to borrow a cart to get my cycle home. The only way I'm gonna get out of being grounded for the rest of my life is if I help you guys warn the town."

Shaun looked at the shack's door and saw that the lock had been torn off, probably so Sam could retrieve a set of golf cart keys. "How were you going to explain the missing golf cart parked at your house?"

Sam sighed. "I was just going to borrow it, dump my bike at home, then bring it back. No one would ever have known it was missing. Everyone is busy at the Founder's Day Festival."

Shaun pictured the festival, the whole town in attendance, all wearing black and yellow, all in danger. He pulled out his phone to see if there was any reception. "Nuts," he said. "No bars."

"That's strange," Toby said. "You can usually get a couple out here."

"Maybe it'll work the closer we get to town," Shaun said, then offered Sam his hand. "Can you make it?"

"I'm good," she said and limped forward, then stopped abruptly, grimacing. "But maybe one of you guys should drive."

"I'll drive," Shaun said. "Stay here and we'll pick you up."

Shaun and Toby ran into the shack and jumped in the front seat of the cart that Sam used to crush the bee. Shaun reached for the key already in the ignition.

"No need," Toby said, pointing at the key. "It's already on. Just hit the gas."

Shaun pressed the accelerator pedal and the cart lurched forward violently into the aluminum wall. They both sat back up and Toby pointed angrily back over the rear seat. "I think we'll get there a lot faster if you go that way, and not through a wall!"

"You said, just hit the gas," Shaun barked back.

"Put it in reverse first, pinhead!"

"Why didn't you say so?" Shaun punched Toby on the shoulder.

Toby returned the punch. "I thought that was obvious, considering there is a giant wall in front of us."

"Oh, my, gawd," Sam yelled. "Please tell me you two aren't planning on being this brain-damaged all day!"

Toby turned around. "We're not *planning* on it."

Shaun put the cart in reverse.

"Go easy," Toby said.

"Bite me," Shaun said, and pressed the accelerator to the floor. The cart lurched back, the electric motor whining. The cart bounced over tools and debris, then shot out of the shack, like a missile from its silo.

"Brake, brake!" Toby yelled as they bounded toward Sam, who looked terrified.

Shaun peered down but didn't see another peddle. "There is no brake!"

"Just take your foot off the accelerator," Toby screamed, as Sam raised her hands.

Shaun lifted his foot, which instantly cut the power. The cart rolled a few more feet, coming to within six inches of Sam before stopping.

Toby took a deep breath and slumped in his seat. "Why, exactly, are you driving?"

"It's okay," Shaun said. "I got it now." He peered back at Sam, who looked as if she'd been holding her breath for a couple of minutes. "Come on, what're you waiting for?"

Sam blinked and lowered her hands. "I'm just trying to decide if I should go with you idiots or just save some time and kill myself now."

Shaun chuckled and held out his hand. "Come on. I know almost exactly, well, kinda-sorta, what I'm doing."

Sam rolled her eyes. "I know I'm gonna regret this." She hopped onto the rear seat, which faced backward. There was a golf bag with a full set of clubs hooked on the rear. Sam propped her injured leg on it.

"Ready?" Shaun asked.

"Does it matter?" Sam said.

"Not really." Shaun hit the accelerator. He made an awkward U-turn then raced down the golf shack's driveway. A few seconds later they were cutting across the rolling fairways and speeding for the exit. When the cart's tires hit the street, they really picked up the pace. Wind whipped through Shaun's hair. He was driving the golf cart at its top speed, and it was moving faster than they could have peddled their bikes. *We're gonna make it*, he thought as they passed the welcome sign that marked the city limits.

Toby tried his phone again, looking frustrated. "I don't understand."

Shaun looked at his friend's phone. "Still nothing?"

Toby shook his head. "No signal."

Shaun pulled his phone out. "Check mine."

Toby examined Shaun's phone. "Same dealeo, man."

"Mine's useless too," Sam said.

Toby handed the phone back to Shaun. "We should get some kind of signal this close to town."

"We're not close to town," Shaun said, turning down the first deserted residential street. "We're in town."

"Where is everybody?" Toby said.

Sam leaned forward. "Everyone is on Main Street."

Shaun glanced at his watch. Sam was right. The festival was well underway, and everybody and their dog was on Main Street, eating cotton candy, playing games, and polishing up the town for the VIPs. And all wearing some form of silly bee costume. To an outsider the festival probably looked like the entire town had gone insane. He had no idea why the mayor thought the festival would impress anyone.

"So what's the plan again?" Sam asked.

Toby turned around and smiled. "Go to town, warn the mayor, become heroes."

"Piece of cake," Shaun said, rounding the final turn onto Main Street. As they straightened out, there was a crunching noise under the tires. Shaun took his foot off the pedal and they all turned around as the cart rolled to a stop.

"Oh, gross," Sam said, pulling her legs more onto her seat.

Behind them was one of the doctor's giant bees. They had run over its head, but by the way it was lying, legs pointed skyward, it was already dead when they hit it. Shaun turned forward and spotted another, and another. *All dead.*

The bees' dead bodies looked like a trail of hideous breadcrumbs leading back up the street to the festival. An icy chill moved through Shaun as he gazed ahead. Nothing moved. An area of town where every resident of Honeywell Springs should be in full celebration mode was completely still. The only thing that moved was a gentle breeze, blowing toward them, carrying a strange and unsettling scent in the air. It smelled like death.

"My god," Shaun said. "We're too late."

CHAPTER

7

YOU ONLY LIVE TWICE

Shaun drove the cart down Main Street. Black and yellow streamers fluttered silently in the breeze overhead as they moved into the festival area. Tables were overturned; cotton candy and popcorn lay on the street as if whoever had been eating them just dropped them where they stood. Lying amongst the abandoned carnival confections were dead bees. Hundreds of dead giant bees.

The golf cart rolled to a stop to the grisly sound of crunching popcorn and insects underneath. Shaun stepped out first, careful not to tread on anything dead. He shuffled ahead, feeling dazed. It was like all the air had been sucked out of his body and his lungs couldn't figure out how to get anymore. He pulled out his inhaler as he glanced up at the elaborate banner spanning the street, reading; *Honeywell Springs' 111th Founders Day Celebration. Buzzing into the Future.*

"Where on Earth is everybody?" Toby said.

Shaun shook his head, then took a squirt from his inhaler. "I guess Dr. Romero was wrong about the bees being slow." He rolled one of the large dead insects over with his foot. Its stinger was gone and its entrails had been ripped out. *It's a terrible way to die*, Shaun remembered his science teacher, Mr. Boothroyd saying. *The bee disembowels itself, all to protect the hive.*

Some of the green ooze had gotten on Shaun's sneaker, and he wiped it on the golf cart's tire. He eyed a puddle of red on the asphalt. Its dark color made it hard to notice, but the more he glanced around the more blood he saw on the street. Human blood.

"I don't like it here, guys," Sam said, her voice shaky. "Getting a bad feeling."

"Hey," Toby said, moving toward the sidewalk. "I found someone."

Shaun followed a few steps behind Toby, who was hurrying toward a pair of thick legs that protruded from beneath an overturned table. Toby grabbed one side of the table. "Let's get this off."

Shaun grabbed the other side and flipped the table into the street. It hit the pavement with a loud slap that echoed like an alarm up and down Main Street. Shaun recognized the man immediately. Only one person in town wore a Monopoly guy-styled top hat, and today it had two large bee antennas attached to the brim.

"It's Mayor Savini," Toby said. He knelt and placed a hand on the five-inch barbed stinger that rose from the mayor's black-and-yellow vest. "Should we pull it out?"

The mayor's eyes were open, staring skyward. In his specially designed black-and-yellow tuxedo, he looked like a giant bee on his way to the prom. Shaun shook his head. "I don't know. What good would it do?"

Toby abruptly stood. "I think I see someone else. I'm gonna go check." Shaun watched his friend step over to the Beeswax Café, where a pudgy hand stuck out over the railing of the dining patio.

"Hey guys," Sam said, still hunkered about twenty feet away in the golf cart.

"Just a sec," Shaun said over his shoulder as he peered back into the dead mayor's eyes. He'd seen characters in movies reach out and close the eyelids of dead bodies dozens of times, but there was no way he was doing that. Still, he couldn't take his gaze away from the mayor's eyes. Something was happening to them.

"It's Carl and his mom," Toby said. "They're dead too."

"Who?" Shaun said, continuing to gaze at the mayor's peepers.

"You know," Toby said. "He's one grade up from us. Won the honeydog-eating contest last year."

Shaun couldn't recall Carl or the contest, but at the moment it didn't matter. What did matter was that the mayor's dead pupils were slowly fading from dark brown to a sickly, milky white.

"Guys," Sam said. "I really think you should take a look at this."

"In a minute," Shaun said. "Hey, Toby. Is anything funky going on with Carl or his mom's eyes?"

"Uh, kind of," Toby said. "How did you—"

"Guys!" Sam screamed.

Shaun stood and it took only a second to see what had alarmed her. Hundreds of townspeople were emerging onto Main Street. They came from all directions, staggering, feet shuffling, arms outstretched, all wearing black and yellow with felt-covered spring antennas bouncing above their dead faces.

Shaun locked eyes with Toby. His friend looked as horrified as Shaun felt. Before either of them could move, Carl and his mom sat up.

"Toby, look out," Shaun yelled.

Wearing a full head-to-toe bumblebee costume, Carl seized Toby's leg. Shaun moved to help Toby, but something grabbed his foot. Trying to keep his balance, Shaun looked down at the mayor. The man's eyes had turned completely white, his mouth was open, and his strong, reanimated hands were pulling Shaun's foot toward his teeth.

"Ahhhh," Shaun screamed and kicked out with his other foot. He fell to the asphalt, landing hard on his butt. He kicked again.

"Get off me, man. Get off me!" Shaun landed a blow to the mayor's face, and the dead man's head snapped back. Amazingly his large top hat stayed affixed to his head as if it had been screwed on, the antennas comically bouncing back and forth. He kicked again, smacking the mayor in the forehead but he didn't let go. Shaun held his breath, reached forward and undid his shoelace. He yanked his foot out of the shoe only a second before the mayor bit into it.

The mayor spit the shoe out and started belly-crawling toward Shaun, growling like a rabid dog. Shaun kicked at the mayor's hands, but one seized him around the ankle. Shaun was about to kick again, when a streak of white zipped into view, smashed into the mayor's temple, and bounced at his feet. It was a golf ball.

The mayor roared with rage or pain, Shaun couldn't tell which. The mayor flipped over onto its back, and Shaun didn't hesitate. He jumped to his feet and immediately turned to help Toby. Carl and his mom, in matching bee costumes, had Toby by the belt loop of his hideous pants. Before Shaun got there a golf ball smashed into Carl's dead face. The heavyset honeydog-eating champion fell back, knocking his mom to the ground. Toby lurched forward and pushed Carl back hard with both hands. Carl staggered and tripped over his mom, and they both rolled on the ground, in a tangle of dead limbs and springing bumblebee antennas.

"Will you dorks get back here," Sam yelled from the cart, clutching a golf ball in each hand.

Shaun sprinted back to the cart. In seconds they were all in, Shaun behind the wheel. He was about to push the accelerator but hesitated. They were surrounded. The reanimated corpses of the citizens of Honeywell Springs were everywhere. Their matching outfits and bee costumes made them look like a dark swarm, closing in all around. Shaun didn't think the cart had enough juice to plow through them, but in a flash he had another idea.

"Hold on," he yelled and floored it. "It's gonna be a tight squeeze."

"What's gonna be a tight squeeze?" Toby said.

Shaun ignored him and aimed the cart toward a gap in the horde between the sidewalk and the honeydog stand. He gunned it at full speed, causing Toby and Sam to hang on tight. The cart tilted as Shaun drove two of its wheels over the curb, then spun the wheel hard, just missing a fire hydrant. The black-and-yellow swarm of zombies moved as a unified organism, attempting to cut off their escape route.

Shaun's heart pounded as he leaned toward Toby, trying to avoid the claw-like hands reaching for him as they sped by. Dead human fingernails scratched along the cart's fiberglass body. They had almost broken free of the horde when something big leaped out of the dunk tank and landed on the front of the cart with a *splat.* It was a round woman, wearing a bee-striped bathing suit, matching swim cap with yellow antennas, and black-tinted pool goggles. She looked like a monstrous water-bug.

The whole cart tilted forward, and Shaun's foot slipped off the accelerator. The cart rolled to a halt.

"Why did you stop!" Sam screamed.

The woman moaned, and brought her face close to Shaun, water from the dunk tank dripping off her dead features.

"Ahhhh," Shaun yelled, "Toby, get it off!"

Toby brought his foot up over the dashboard and was about to kick the zombie, but stopped. "Hey, it's Ms. Barbara, our kindergarten teacher."

"Dude, I don't care who it is!"

The reanimated woman wrapped her cold, wet hands around Shaun's throat.

"I don't think she wants to go over our ABCs right now!" Shaun yelled.

"I can't kick our kindergarten teacher, man!" Toby said.

Ms. Barbara squeezed Shaun's neck, bringing her teeth close to his face.

"Dude!" Shaun pleaded.

"Ahhhh!" Toby kicked Ms. Barbara in the forehead.

The kindergarten teacher rolled off the front of the cart and hit the street with a wet *thud!*

"Oh, that's not right," Toby said.

Shaun took a deep breath and pushed the pedal to the floor. "Thanks, man."

"Sorry, Ms. Barbara," Toby yelled over his shoulder as they sped away. "I'm gonna get expelled for that, I just know it."

Shaun did his best to shake it off. He gripped the wheel tightly and pushed harder on the accelerator, wishing the stupid electric cart could go faster. He spun the wheel, turning off Main Street into an alley he and Toby had used as a shortcut walking home from elementary school. The alley led to an access road that let out just two blocks from their houses.

"Hey, where are you going?" Sam yelled in Shaun's ear.

They zipped down the narrow alleyway. "We used to go this way…" Shaun saw what a huge mistake he'd just made. "Oh, crap."

He had forgotten that sometime last year they had built a Rent-a-Space storage facility that blocked the other end of the alley.

"Oh, that's just great!" Sam said. "Nicely done, dweeb!"

Shaun felt horrible. He had driven them not toward safety, but into a dead-end corridor of death.

"I forgot they built that thing too," Toby said. "I'd have done the same thing."

"Thanks, Toby," Shaun said as he drove to the end of the alley and brought the cart to a stop next to the twenty-foot-high wall that wasn't there a year ago.

"You think we can climb it," Toby said.

Shaun scanned the three walls around them. They had nothing to hold on to. "We can't even climb that stupid rope in gym class."

"Speak for yourself," Sam said, hobbling out of the cart. She limped for a yard then bent over, clutching her knee. She leaned on a large industrial dumpster that had its lids raised against the wall. "On second thought."

A collective moan echoed down the alley. They all turned around. A hundred zombies dressed as giant bees spilled into the alley like army ants invading a burrow. Their springy antennas pointed the way as they shambled toward the golf cart. It would take the swarm only minutes to reach them.

"What now, geniuses?" Sam said.

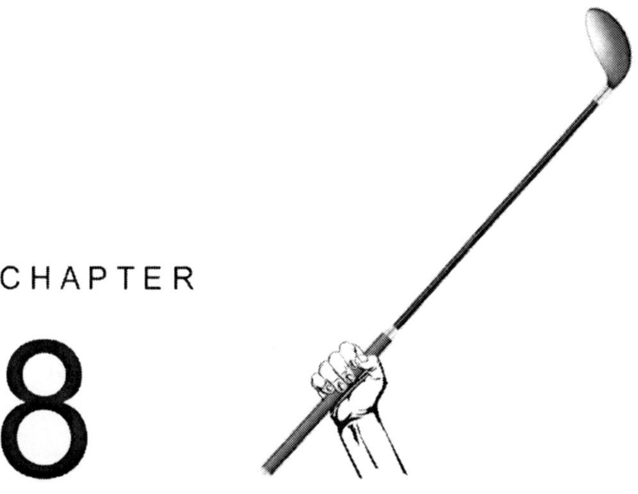

CHAPTER

8

DIE ANOTHER DAY

They scanned the alley for an exit. Nothing. Not a door, window, drainage pipe to climb on, no fire escape or balconies. Nothing. Just solid wall going straight up on three sides.

"I can't believe this is happening." Pressure built in Shaun's chest as the zombie swarm closed the final forty yards between them.

Sam pushed away from the dumpster, its open lids scraping on the wall behind it. She hobbled over to the cart. Looking in the golf bag, she pulled out a club, then rested it on her shoulder like a batter coming up to the plate. Clearly, she was prepared to fight.

With the hundreds of undead stumbling toward them, Shaun knew that one girl with a golf club didn't stand much of a chance. He forced himself to take a breath, and surprisingly he was able to get a good deep fill of air. He walked over to the golf cart, looked over at Sam and grabbed a club. *If this is the end, at least we'll go out swinging.*

"You two gonna take on the whole town?" Toby said.

"Yes," Sam snapped, decidedly. "You gotta problem with that?"

"Well, I don't think your gonna kill a lot of zombies with those."

Sam looked at her club. "What's wrong with it?"

"It's a sand wedge," Toby said, then pointed at Shaun's club. "And that's a putter."

"What does it matter?" Shaun said.

"You can't effectively fight zombies with a sand wedge and a putter," Toby said. "There's a proper club for every situation."

Shaun tossed the putter. "Fine, Tiger Woods, what do you suggest?"

Toby narrowed his eyes. "I suggest you *not* turn down a dead-end alley!"

"Oh, that's helpful, Toby," Shaun snapped.

"Will you guys shut up." Sam tossed the sand wedge to the ground, then held out a hand to Toby. "What's the right club for this situation?"

Toby looked thoughtful for a moment as dead moans echoed in the alley. He then reached in the bag and quickly pulled out three clubs. Sam got a seven wood, and Shaun a five iron. Toby kept the three iron for himself. As Shaun brought up the new club, he had to admit, it felt a lot more deadly than the putter.

"I'm sorry, Toby," Shaun said.

Toby smiled, bringing up his club. "Me too."

"For what it's worth," Shaun said, "it's been pretty awesome being your friend."

"Best friends," Toby added.

"My gawd," Sam said. "If you dweebs hug, I will so throw up."

Standing shoulder to shoulder with Sam in the middle, the three stared straight ahead at the shambling black-and-yellow horde not more than twenty yards away. Shaun could see their milky white eyes, empty and hungry. Their mouths hung open as if they wanted to waste no time opening them before biting.

Shaun looked away and tried not to image what the next few moments of his short life were going to be like. His gaze fell on the dumpster to his right along with the strange sense that they had overlooked something. *Why would there be a dumpster here if the alley has no access? How do they take out the trash?*

Shaun scanned the alley again. He remembered watching garbage trucks as a kid. Sometimes when they slammed these big dumpsters down, they rolled in all kinds of ways. He'd even seen one roll into a parked car once. He dropped to his knees and peered under the bottom on the dumpster.

"Dude, you okay?" Toby said.

Shaun could see completely underneath the dumpster—all the way

to the wall. *Eureka!*

Shaun jumped to his feet. "Help me move this thing!"

"Why?" Sam said.

Shaun gripped the massive frame of the metal bin. "Because there's a door behind it!"

Sam and Toby dropped their clubs.

"Jeez," Toby said. "With the lids up, we couldn't see it."

They rolled the dumpster back far enough to access the door. But there was another problem.

"Damn," Shaun said. "There's no handle."

"It only opens from the inside," Sam said.

"Okay, now what?" Sam said as they all looked at the swarm now only five yards away.

Shaun got an idea. "Come on, help me push this forward."

"Why?" Sam said.

"No time!" Shaun snapped, taking charge.

They rolled the dumpster perpendicular to the side walls, butting one end against the bricks and the other against the golf cart. In just a few seconds, they'd created a barricade. A gap remained between the opposite side wall and the golf cart, but it was narrow. The zombies would have to squeeze through one at a time.

"That should buy us some time to get the door open," Shaun said.

Sam's face glimmered with hope. "It's a good thing you're smarter than you look."

The undead horde hit the dumpster with a hollow metallic thud. The bin started rolling back.

"Lock the wheels!" Toby screamed. Using their feet, Sam and Toby kicked down the levers, latching the wheels in place.

"Now what," Sam said.

Shaun pointed to the thin gap in the barricade by the golf cart. Zombies were already moving toward it. "You guys hold them off. I'll work on the door."

Toby and Sam gathered their golf clubs. Shaun ran to the door and tried to wedge his fingers into the crevice around the lock. Nothing doing. The space was too narrow. *I need something to stick in there*, he thought.

Shaun spun around. Toby and Sam stood at the gap in their barricade, clubs held high. A half dozen zombies were trying to force their way through at the same time, all getting stuck, their springy bee antennas bouncing on the golf cart's roof. "Guys, I need a thin piece of metal."

Sam kept an eye on the zombies while Toby searched the golf cart. He tossed out short eraserless pencils, score cards, then shook his head at Shaun. Shaun dashed to the dumpster and peered inside. It contained only a few garbage bags, but in the far corner lay scraps of metal.

"I'm on it," Toby said, leaping from the cart and into the refuse bin.

"Whatever you dweebs are going to do," Sam said over her shoulder, "do it fast!"

The zombies were no longer stuck in a bottleneck. They inched forward one at a time into the gap. Several had figured out that they didn't need to go around the golf cart—they could climb through it. One had already crawled over the back seat, and Shaun's heart skipped a beat as he recognized the undead man wrapped in a black-and-yellow apron, broken antennas sprouting from his fiery hair. *Mr. Hooper!*

Sam swung her club. With a smack, it connected with the head of the first zombie to work its way through the gap. It staggered forward, then dropped to its knees, a thick greenish ooze spilling down its forehead.

"Dude, heads up," Toby yelled.

Shaun glanced over in time to see a long hunk of metal flying his way. He snatched it out of the air, then spun back to the door. In an instant he realized it was too thick. "Find another one," Shaun said. "A little thinner!"

"It's not really a hardware store in here, man!"

"Dude!"

"Okay!" Toby dived back in. He came up a second later with a thin metal rod and tossed it to Shaun.

"Excellent." Shaun caught it, then quickly thrust it into the door's crevice. It slipped in but he needed to wedge it in further for leverage.

"Shaun, look out!" Toby yelled.

Shun spun around and came face to face with Mr. Hooper. The boss's milky white gaze bore into him as he reached for Shaun's throat. Shaun ducked. Mr. Hooper's dead claws narrowly missed his face.

"Shaun!" Toby tossed his three iron into the air.

Shaun grabbed it, dropped to one knee, and swung it as hard as he could. Mr. Hooper was a heavy man who always complained about his weak knees. Shaun hoped they caused him as much trouble in death as they had in life. The head of the three iron hit the big man's right knee, and the zombie dropped like a piano. Immediately, it began to get up.

"I'm real sorry about this, Mr. Hooper," Shaun brought the club up.

"It's all in the follow-through, dude," Toby said from the dumpster.

Shaun swung the club like a PGA pro. He hit Mr. Hooper on the bridge of the nose, and his head snapped back as Shaun followed through with his swing. The big man slumped forward, green gunk dripping from his bent nose.

Shaun looked over at Sam. Three zombies lay unmoving at her feet, but another was reaching for her. Shaun was about to turn back to the door, when Toby let out a scream.

A zombie had thrust its arm through the golf cart and grabbed a hold of Toby's sweater. Shaun started toward him, but Toby shouted, "I'm okay, just get that door open."

Shaun hesitated. Then he turned, raised the club, and brought it down on the end of the rod he'd stuck in the door. He pounded it several more times like someone hammering a railroad spike. Thinking it was in far enough, he threw his weight into the rod, pushing as hard as he could. Metal tore, and there was a soft ping as the door popped open.

Shaun thrust his hand inside. "Got it!" He looked back in time to see Sam take a swing. A female zombie in full bumblebee costume slumped against the wall, green slime decorating the alley. Sam turned and ran to the door.

"Toby, come on!" Shaun screamed.

Toby had managed to get away from the hand that seized him from inside the golf cart, but two more had come over the top of the dumpster. One had a hold of his hair, the other his sleeve. Shaun was about to rush over, but Sam grabbed hold of his collar and pulled him inside the door. Shaun stumbled back and landed on the tile floor inside the building. Lying flat on his back, he watched helplessly as Sam slammed the door shut.

Shaun jumped up. "Toby is still out there!"

CHAPTER

9

LIVE AND LET DIE

"Get out of my way," Shaun said. The sounds of zombies pounding on the alley side of the door echoed down the corridor.

Sam stood her ground in front of the door clutching her golf club. "Look, I know you guys were *besties* and all, but you're not opening that door."

Shaun narrowed his eyes. "Those things will tear Toby apart. Now get out of my way!"

Sam leaned back on the door and shook her head. "Open this door, and they'll do the same to us."

Shaun sighed, considering what to do. Sam was a few inches taller and probably outweighed him by twenty pounds. If he tried to get by her physically, he'd probably lose. He had to try something else. "He wouldn't leave *you* out there."

"How do you know?"

"Whose idea do you think it was to go check on you at the golf cart shack? Not mine. I don't give a zombie's butt what happens to you."

"I was fine," Sam snapped. "Didn't need rescuing from you dorks."

"Ah, newsflash!" Shaun screamed. "You, were in, a *treeeee*!"

Sam's voice softened. "Why would he come looking for me?"

Shaun rolled his eyes. "Who the heck knows? I don't understand half the things he does. The weird pants obsession… No clue, man. No frickin' clue. But he's my best friend, and for some demented reason he likes *you!*"

Sam looked as if she'd just been slapped. "How… does… what do you mean?"

"He *likes* you."

Sam shook her head. "You're not serious."

"I think he needs to have his eyes examined, but for whatever reason, Toby thinks you're cute."

Sam's cheeks suddenly became flush with color. "Really?"

Shaun rolled his eyes, then pushed Sam aside. She didn't resist.

Leaning forward, Shaun opened the door a crack. Black-and-yellow zombies were everywhere, bumping into one another, moaning, clawing at the walls, and searching. Through an opening in the horde he saw the dumpster about ten feet away. He smiled. Toby had somehow managed to get the dumpster lids closed, and he knew his friend was inside. *Safe.*

Shaun held still and waited for the zombies to stagger far enough away from the door so he could try to get Toby's attention. But before they did, one of the dumpster lids rose slowly. A pair of eyes peered out from the crack.

"Can you see him?" Sam asked softly behind Shaun.

"Ya," Shaun said. "But I bet he doesn't smell real good."

"How are we gonna get him in here?"

"Maybe if we wait long enough, the zombies will get bored, and go eat somebody else." But even as he said it, Shaun knew that wouldn't happen for a long while. More zombies were continuing to squeeze in one at a time through the thin space between the wall and the golf cart. The end of the alley looked like an overcrowded elevator, with the dead standing shoulder to shoulder. Soon there would be so many bee-costumed zombies, he would be unable to open the door.

If we're going to have a chance at getting him, Shaun thought, *it has to be now. But how?*

Before he could think of anything, Toby stuck out a paper plate. It was torn and caked half in mustard, but in the area that was still white, Toby had written something. Shaun squinted to read it. *Live and Let Die.*

Sam peered over Shaun's head at Toby's message. "Live and let die," she whispered. "What the heck does that mean?"

Shaun met Toby's gaze and gave him a nod. Toby returned the nod, held up a finger and mouthed the words, *one minute.*

Shaun let the door close and shut his eyes, picturing the alligator scene from the movie *Live and Let Die.*

"Well," Sam said, "what does it mean?"

"It means," Shaun said, "that Toby is about to do something really stupid."

Sam grabbed Shaun by the shoulder and spun him around. "Explain."

"Have you ever seen a James Bond movie?"

"Who hasn't?"

"Toby and I have seen every one, more than ten times each. Except the ones with Pierce Brosnan. Those blow."

Sam looked impatient. "Is there a point on its way?"

"In *Live and Let Die*, James Bond is trapped but escapes by walking across a pond full of alligators."

"How does he do—"

"Bond steps on the alligator's heads and walks to safety."

Sam paused for a moment. "So… your idiot friend is going to… oh, that *is* stupid."

"That's Toby," Shaun said.

"When is he going to attempt this stupid stunt?'

From outside they heard a sudden burst of noise, as the dumpster lids flew open.

"Like, now," Shaun said. He opened the door a crack and saw Toby hunkered toward the back of the dumpster. Toby stood up and pounded his chest like King Kong.

"Hey you, dead, ugly, flesh-eating monsters," Toby yelled. "Come get some grade-A Toby, all you can eat!"

It took a moment for Shaun to figure out what Toby was doing, but as all the zombies in the alley turned their attention toward the dumpster, it became clear. Toby was drawing them close, so close that they were all pressed up against the dumpster's metal sides, tight, several zombies deep. *Hopefully tight enough to walk on.*

Toby stayed just out of reach, continuing to wave his arms and be obnoxious. Not only did this bring the undead toward him but it cleared the area around the door.

"You want some of this?" Toby taunted, slapping his belly. "Oh, yeah, how about you?"

The dumpster suddenly jolted, as a zombie inadvertently unlocked one of the wheels. The whole thing started to roll away from the door, and Shaun felt a rush of panic.

"Time to go!" Toby leaped up onto the dumpster's edge. Without hesitation, he stepped out onto the head on the first zombie, and quickly stepped forward to the next. In four long strides, he had cleared the field of zombies, but as he neared the door, there were no more undead to walk on.

Shaun flung the door open wide. It smacked the alley wall and Toby leaped stuntman-style into the opening. He sailed clear over Shaun and landed on Sam. The two tumbled to the ground in a tangled heap of limbs and grunts. Shaun stepped out and grabbed the door to shut it.

A second before the door closed, a zombie thrust its dead fingers inside the door frame. Shaun pulled the door, hard. With a grotesque cracking the door slammed shut. Three dismembered fingers dropped to the floor at his feet. "Ah, nasty," he said, kicking a slimy digit away.

Sam groaned behind him. Shaun turned and saw her push Toby off of her. Toby sat up against the corridor wall, panting. "Dude, did you see me? Did you see what I did?"

Shaun knelt next to him, nodding.

"Good," Toby said. "Because I am *never* doing that again!"

"That was so 007, man," Shaun said.

Toby took a deep breath. "That's me, double-O-Toby."

"I'm glad you're not dead and all, double-O-dweeb." Sam got to her feet. "But next time, find someone else to land on."

Toby snapped off a salute. "Roger that."

Sam rolled her eyes. "I gotta pee," she said, then stormed off down the corridor.

Toby leaned toward Shaun. "Did you hear that?"

"What?"

Toby raised his brow. "She's *glad* I'm not dead."

"So am I, what's your point?"

"Dude, I think she's starting to notice me."

"You just landed on her, man," Shaun said, standing up. "How could she not notice you?" He held a hand down to his friend. Toby took it and pulled himself up. They stood in the corridor watching as Sam turned out of sight.

"Where are we exactly?" Toby said.

They started after Sam. "The alley goes between the Honeywell Community Theater and the Main Street Department Store. Does that sound right?" Shaun said.

Toby nodded. "But which one are we in?"

The corridor ended, and they stepped into a large room with racks of clothes.

"This doesn't look like the theater," Shaun said.

The Main Street Department Store was a three-story building with the bottom floor dedicated to women's fashions. They stood at the rear of the store. Toby reached over and picked up a delicate piece of cloth, hot pink and about the size of a coaster. Others just like it, in a variety of patterns were spread out on the counter.

"So we would be in…" Toby said looking at the cloth, puzzled.

"The lingerie department." Shaun picked up a hanger. The undergarment that dangled from it looked like a cross between a slingshot and one of the fancy napkins Shaun's mom puts out at Thanksgiving. He held it up so Toby could see. "Do girls really wear this stuff?"

Toby grinned. "Man, I hope so."

Sam came out of the restroom, the sound of a flushed toilet fading in the background. Shaun turned toward her. "Hey, Sam. You're sort of a girl. Do you wear stuff like this?"

Sam narrowed her eyes. "Pervs." Clearly disgusted, she headed to the front of the store.

"I take it that's a big *no*," Shaun said and tossed the garment. He spied a phone on the other side of the counter next to a cash register. He picked up the receiver.

"Anything?" Toby said.

Shaun shook his head. "Dead as disco, man."

"What the hell, dude? Why aren't the phones working?"

"No clue," Shaun said, beginning to suspect that something beside zombies was plaguing them. "Let's catch up with Sam."

Shaun and Toby followed Sam to the front of the store, making turn after turn through the clothes racks like rats in a maze. When they finally joined her, Sam stood at the main entrance, gazing out the glass double doors. The store's entire frontage was mostly glass, and looking out Shaun felt a little bit like a fish in an aquarium.

"You weren't thinking of going out there?" Shaun said to Sam.

She shook her head. "I was just wondering what they were doing."

"Who?" Toby said.

Sam pointed. "Them."

The zombies, some with wings fashioned from wire and black netting, were all staggering to the sidewalks, then doing the oddest thing. They hunched in the shadows of abandoned concession stands, sat down behind shrubs, and lingered around alleyway corners. At first Shaun thought they were trying to get out of the sunlight, but the sun was low in the sky, nearing sunset, and most of the street was already in shadow.

Then Shaun remembered when they had stepped out of the golf cart onto Main Street, how one minute it was quiet and the next….

Sam said, "It's almost as if…"

"They're hiding," Shaun mumbled, finishing Sam's thought.

"Hiding?" Toby said. "Zombies don't hide."

"It would explain how they seem to come at us suddenly from everywhere," Shaun said. "Remember, one second the street was dead quiet, then in the next it was dead alive."

"So, you're a zombie expert now?" Toby said.

Shaun sighed. "Dude."

"Exactly how many zombie movies have you seen," Toby said. "Oh, yeah, I know. None."

"Okay, snot-wad," Shaun said, folding his arms. "What're they doing?"

"Well," Toby said, rubbing his chin. "Looks like they're hiding."

Shaun threw his hands in the air. "Brilliant. I wish I'd thought of that."

Sam rolled her head back and sighed, then seemed to speak to the ceiling. "Why didn't I just stay at the golf course and find a nice pleasant way to kill myself? Anything is better than listening to you two idiots."

"Okay, butt-munch," Toby said to Shaun. "What're they hiding from?"

"I don't—" Shaun's words cut off as a column of black limousines slowly rolled into view. At least three drove in front of the store, black windows concealing their occupants. The vehicles slowed, then stopped.

"It's the VIPs," Sam said.

"Oh, man," Toby said. "It's gonna be an ambush."

CHAPTER

10

A VIEW TO A KILL

Leaving their vehicles idling, all the limo drivers got out at once and immediately started opening the passenger doors.

"They'll be torn to pieces." Shaun moved toward the store front. As the VIPs began stepping out, looking a little confused, Shaun pounded on the glass. "Get back inside!"

A chauffeur looked over at Shaun, bewildered, as he held the door open for his passengers. Soon there were twenty or so, well-dressed men and women standing in the deserted street, looking around for signs of life. Shaun ran to the front door, but it was locked, closed early for Founder's Day. He scanned the door frame and spotted a manual deadbolt lever. He gave it a twist and pushed the glass door open. "Get inside!"

A heavyset man in an aqua-blue dress shirt said, "Young man, where is everybody?"

"Dead," Shaun yelled. "They're all dead, and you're next if you don't get back in the car!"

The man smiled as if Shaun had told a bad joke. "Would you just tell Mayor Savini that we're here? He's expecting us."

A scream came from the rear limo. The black-and-yellow zombies had started their attack. At first the VIPs just stood there. They were dazed or perhaps thought that the costumed walking dead with novelty bee antennas and flapping insect wings were part of some welcoming show. But when the zombies began to come out of hiding and surrounded the limos, they all screamed.

The VIPs had nowhere to run. A few tried to dive back into the limos, but the undead townsfolk of Honeywell Springs dragged them out, dropped them in the street then dog-piled on top. Shaun closed the door and turned away.

Toby walked up to Shaun and peered out at the carnage.

"Why didn't they listen to me?" There was a touch of sadness in Shaun's voice. "All they had to do was get back in their freaking cars."

"Don't beat yourself up, Shaun," Toby said. "You know grown ups don't listen to kids."

Shaun looked back outside. There were too many black-and-yellow dressed zombies to all feed on the VIPs, and many began to wander off. Some staggered toward the department store, eyes wide, springy bee antennas bouncing over their dead heads. Shaun began to associate names with the undead faces. "That's Ms. Kindle the librarian," he said, remembering that he owed her at least two bucks in overdue book fees. "And there's Casey Tarman. She did that cool honeycomb mural last year in the school cafeteria."

"Hey, isn't that Freddy Mathews?" Toby said.

"No that's his twin, Joey," Shaun corrected. "Freddy is over there, gnawing on that foot."

Toby nodded. "I could never tell them apart, dead or alive. Hey, isn't that Alice Honeychile?"

Shaun felt a flutter at the mention of her name. "Where?"

Toby pointed across the street where a thin girl, wearing black leotards, yellow bumblebee wings, and antennas sticking out of a beehive hairdo, was eating human fingers like French fries.

Shaun recognized the red curls that had come loose from her cone-shaped hair as her jaw violently crushed her meal. "Yeah, that's Alice," he said.

"You had a crush on her last summer, remember?" Toby said.

Shaun sighed. "No I didn't."

"Yeah, you did. Remember you used to make us ride bikes by her house after soccer practice, so—"

"Okay," Shaun said. "Maybe a little."

"Alice Honeychile?" Sam said with a sneer in her voice. "A dweeb like you wouldn't have a chance with Alice."

"Nobody asked you," Shaun barked.

"Sam's right," Toby said. "Alice was way out of your league." Toby cocked his head as if to take another look at the zombie formerly known as Alice Honeychile, now on bended knee fighting with another zombie over what looked like an eyeball. "But now, maybe you got a shot."

"Dude," Shaun snapped. "Don't be gross."

"Naw," Sam said with a chuckle, as zombie Alice popped the slimly eye into her mouth like a big gumball. "She's still out of your league."

Toby and Sam chuckled.

Shaun looked up at Sam, whose smiling face loomed about three inches over his. "Look, Sasquatch, no one is talking to you."

Sam shook her head dismissively as Shaun turned back to the street. "Just look at them, man. They were our neighbors, family, and friends. Now look at them."

"You think the whole world is like this?" Toby said.

"I don't know," Shaun said. "Might explain why the phones don't work."

"Hey, dweeb," Sam said.

"What?" Shaun answered, somehow knowing which dweeb she meant.

"Did you relock the door after trying to do your hero thing, warning the VIPs?"

"No, why?" Shaun glanced at the door and beyond. Several zombies were staring at them, and two others were probing the store's glass door, grasping the outside handle and pulling.

"Damn," Shaun muttered. "Sorry, my bad."

One of Sheriff Rosco's deputies, wearing spring-mounted bee antennas and his black-and-yellow uniform from the ladies auxiliary, needed to use both hands but managed to pull the door open. Another zombie stepped forward and used its body to force the door wide enough to stick open, permanently.

"Time to go," Sam said, already turning away.

"Where," Toby shouted, running after her.

"Up," Shaun yelled as he trailed behind, zigzagging through the racks, his lungs beginning to tighten.

"What?" Toby shouted.

Shaun tried to repeat it, but he couldn't catch a breath. He switched the golf club to his left hand in order to pull his inhaler from his pocket with his right. He pumped a fast squirt. Instantly his lungs relaxed, and he took a breath. He scanned for Toby, and found his friend staring at him, eyes wide.

"Shaun, look out!"

A hand seized Shaun's shoulder and whirled him around. The Honeywell Springs deputy towered over him like a rotting oak tree. Off-balance, Shaun swung his golf club. By some miracle, it connected with the dead lawman's jaw, knocking him back a step, but the motion spun Shaun's feet out from under him. He toppled back into a table. Its contents slid off onto Shaun as he hit the floor.

Covered in large pieces of cloth, Shaun frantically slapped them off his face. The deputy knelt down, fingers glistening with blood, and reached for Shaun's throat. Shaun went to swing the golf club, but his hands were full of ladies garments. The deputy opened his mouth close enough to Shaun's face that he could see pieces of meat and gore in the man's teeth.

With nothing else at his disposal, Shaun thrust one of the garments toward the open mouth. The cloth unfolded in front of him, giving him an idea. Shaun quickly slapped the extra-large pair of ladies underwear over the zombie's head. The deputy's bee antennas stuck up through the leg holes, and the large elastic waistband hung down over his mouth, dangling on his neck like a fat man's chin.

Blinded, the zombie scratched at his face, trying to figure out how to remove the underwear. Shaun crab-crawled backward, but after a few feet bumped into a pair of legs. He looked up into Ms. Kindle's twisted face. She reached down and grabbed Shaun by the hair and wrenched him up.

Shaun gazed into her milk-white, crazed, hungry eyes. She wanted something from him, but it wasn't his overdue book fees. It was flesh.

Shaun snatched another baggy pair of underwear off his shoulder as Ms. Kindle's mouth came toward his face. He slapped the elastic-lined cloth over her head. It didn't blind her—she could see with one dead eye through a leg hole—but her mouth was covered. Shaun felt her teeth on his cheek, trying to take a bite but unable to get hold of enough skin to clamp down on.

The librarian zombie howled in frustration, releasing Shaun in order to try and uncover her head. Shaun stumbled back feeling more hands at his back. He frantically spun around, picked underwear off his body and slapped them over the zombie's heads, doing his best to cover their eyes and mouths. He was surrounded, but he had a plan, and a lot of underwear.

After covering five more dead heads, bee antennas poking up from the leg holes, Shaun pushed his way through them, found some daylight, then zigzagged through the racks to where Toby waited at the bottom of the unmoving escalator.

Out of breath, Shaun leaned over, one hand on his knee, the other on the escalator's rubber hand-rail. He felt Toby enthusiastically slap him on his back.

"Dude, you're officially my new hero."

Shaun tried to straighten up. "What?" he said, trying to catch his breath.

"You just defeated a horde of zombies with granny panties, man. Never would have believed that if I hadn't seen it."

Shaun slowly stood up straight as Sam yelled.

"Hey, dweebs, move your butts."

Sam stood at the top of the escalator, about to step onto the second floor. She was pointing back into the store behind them.

"Ah, man." Toby grabbed Shaun by the arm and pulled him up the steps. Halfway between the floors, they stopped and looked back. Zombies rolled toward them in waves. The dead didn't bother going around the clothes racks; they just washed right over them like the tide coming in. There had to be hundreds flooding through the ladies department, all moving toward the escalator.

"Ah, jeez." Toby's voice trembled. "We're gonna need a *lot* more ladies underwear."

CHAPTER

11

NEVER SAY NEVER AGAIN

Shaun and Toby leaped up onto the second floor.

"Okay, now what?" Sam said. "Do we keep going up?"

Shaun looked around. He was nauseated and his hands were shaking—both side effects from overuse of his inhaler—but his mind remained focused. "Second floor, menswear, sporting goods and toys, right?"

"Yeah," Toby said.

Shaun glanced down the escalator and estimated he had at least two minutes before the zombies swarmed up the unmoving steps, and hit the second floor.

"All right, you guys stay here and hold them off." Shaun turned and moved into the store.

"Hold them off," Sam called. "How do we do that?"

Shaun shouted back over his shoulder. "You're right by the toys. Just chuck things at them. It should slow them down."

"Where're you going," Toby yelled.

"Shopping!" Shaun skidded around a corner on his sock, then darted to the shoe department. He snatched sneakers, checking the size. Everything was too big and he didn't have time to hunt through the back room for a good fit, so he grabbed some Teva outdoor sandals. They didn't look like the right size either, but they were adjustable. He kicked off his shoe and slapped them on. With his socks on it was a decent fit.

He sprinted two aisles over into sporting goods. Having lost his golf club in a pile of ladies underwear, he needed a new weapon. He hoped for a baseball bat, hockey stick or even another golf club, but the aisle he turned down was full of tennis gear. He paused for a moment wondering if he should continue the hunt, but he heard commotion from back at the escalator. Sam and Toby had started chucking toys down the steps which meant the zombies were close.

Shaun grabbed a metal racquet. He'd never played tennis in his life, didn't even know how to grip the racquet, but he figured when it came to smashing zombies in the head, a game-perfect grip wasn't important. He was about to head back when something caught his eye. A slingshot. Why slingshots were stocked next to tennis balls, was something to ponder.

"Shaun, hurry it up, man!" Toby sounded panicked.

With a pounding heart, Shaun snatched a slingshot, a packet of pellets, and then took off. Ten seconds later he was back at the escalator, stepping behind Sam as she hurled a large Fisher Price kitchen sink and oven down the steps.

Toby threw his hands in the air. "She shoots, she scores!"

The large box smashed into Ms. Kindle, who toppled back into the line of zombies behind her. They fell like rotting dominoes, all landing in a black-and-yellow pile of tangled antennas and bent bumblebee wings.

"How's it going?" Shaun said.

"It was touch and go there for a minute," Toby said. "We started off hurling action figures, which really just annoyed them. But then Sam found the big toddler stuff and it was like bowling for zombies, man."

"Let's go up to the third floor," Shaun said.

"Why?" Sam asked, picking up an Easy-Bake Oven.

"Yeah," Toby said. "Why don't we just stay here and clog up the escalator with this stuff?"

"There's better stuff upstairs," Shaun said.

"What's up there?" Toby asked.

"Furniture department."

After lifting the floral-print love seat into place atop the pile of furniture clogging the escalator, Toby and Shaun collapsed, placing their backs against the metal railing. Exhausted, Shaun peered down and saw zombies attempting to crawl over the mounds of furniture. The undead didn't have the dexterity or coordination to maneuver over the huge obstacle, and several slid off at mid-point, crashing to the floor below. If they hadn't already been dead they surely would have been after slamming through glass display cases, headfirst.

"There goes another one," Toby said, as a zombie toppled backward, its bumblebee costume momentarily hanging it up. A large foam-rubber stinger snagged on an end table Sam had hurled down. When the zombie finally fell over the railing, the undersized wings attached to the back of its costume fluttered uselessly, clearly demonstrating that bees really shouldn't fly. The zombie hit the floor with a loud *splat.*

"They'll never get through that," Sam said.

Shaun felt a real sense of relief. There might not be a whole lot of supplies up here, but they could definitely hold out until help arrived. *If help arrived.* He glanced again at the stairs, piled high with furniture. His stomach tightened with a rising dread. With the escalators not moving it was easy to think of them as stairs. Up or down, two-way traffic—that was how stairs worked. But these were not stairs! They were escalators, with one set of steps going up and another set going down.

Shaun jumped to his feet.

Toby eyed his friend. "What is it?"

Shaun gazed around the furniture department. "Where's the other escalator?"

"Other escalator?" Toby said, his face scrunching.

Pounding a fist on the rubber hand rail, Shaun shouted, "This one goes down, where's the one coming up?"

Toby leaped to his feet and the two boys took off, sprinting toward the front of the store. They jumped over mattresses in the bedding department, zigzagged through lamps in lighting, and darted around washers, refrigerators and ovens in appliances. When they arrived at the up escalator, Shaun felt instantly relieved. No zombies in sight. But then they could see the fuzzy puffball tips of bumblebee antennas bouncing into view.

From the top of the escalator, they could see that a zombie swarm was two-thirds of the way up, shoulder to shoulder, almost fighting each other to reach the top. Shaun looked around for something large to hurl down, but they were surrounded by candles and picture frames, with smiling black-and-white photos of happy people doing something other than running for their lives from zombies.

"Should we go get some stuff?" Toby said. "Those appliances aren't that far away."

Shaun knew the distance was much too far. "We'd never make it, and I don't think we could move a refrigerator."

"I could move a house if it would keep them down there." Toby looked at Shaun. "So now what?"

"Maybe we can get to the roof?"

Toby's eyes lit up. "There are emergency stairs by the elevator. I think they lead to the roof."

"How do you know that?"

"My dad was called in a few years ago to fix the elevator. Mom was out of town, so I went with, and—"

"Okay, okay," Shaun said. "Which way?"

Toby pointed back the way they had come, then took off running. Shaun stayed right on his heels. As they sprinted from the candle section, they saw Sam coming the other way, her limp noticeably worse.

Shaun and Toby waved and yelled. "Go back! Go back!"

"Why?" Sam shouted angrily.

They stopped and Shaun pointed behind them, as zombies stepped onto the third floor. The first two were so close to one another their bee antennas got tangled.

"Ah, man." Sam came to a hobbling stop next to Shaun.

They could see how bad Sam was hurt. The area around her knee was purple and swollen to the size of a grapefruit.

Sam spun around and started heading back the other way, just as Shaun caught the sympathetic look in Toby's eye. Toby rushed up behind Sam and grabbed her arm, throwing it over his shoulder. Shaun rolled his eyes, knowing he couldn't let his friend take on the annoying burden that was Samantha Campbell all by *himself.* Shaun grabbed the other arm and flung it over his shoulder. Sam resisted at first, but when the two boys lifted her up and started moving at twice her speed, she gave in.

They were at the elevator in less than a minute, only stumbling once when Sam attempted to lead. When they arrived, Shaun saw two doorways without doors. One led to the emergency stairs, the other to what looked like a break room. Probably where employees ate meals when working their shifts.

"You and Sam head to the roof," Shaun said. "I'll meet you up there."

"Where're you…" Toby said, but Shaun had already stepped away. He darted into the break room, hoping there might be a working refrigerator where employees stored their lunchboxes. Shaun wasn't hungry, but even a mini fridge might have some ice to help Sam's swelling leg. If the damaged tissue got any worse, Sam was really going to slow them down, and Shaun had the feeling that Toby wouldn't leave her behind, no matter how big a pain in the butt she was.

Score! The break room had a full-size fridge. Shaun snagged two ice trays, tucked them under an arm, then headed back out. Before running to the stairs he stopped to check how far the zombies had advanced. His jaw dropped. They were closer than he'd imagined. They had surged all the way into the bedding department, where many of them staggered into mattresses, fell forward then scurried on all fours. Dressed as bees they already appeared as macabre human-sized insects, but watching them crawl like infectious roaches sent a shiver up Shaun's spine.

He spun around and made a beeline for the emergency stairs. In the stairwell, he paused and leaned over the railing, peering down. He could see all the way to the first floor, but more importantly he could see the zombies swarming up the stairwell. Even if they had blocked both escalators, the zombies still would have been able to get to them.

A chill moved through Shaun as he realized they might have been relaxing in leather easy chairs, thinking they were safe, as zombies snuck up the back stairwell. If that had happened there would have been nowhere to go. Nowhere to run. *Game over.*

Up he went. Shaun took the steps two at a time, rounding the stairwell, hoping to see Toby and Sam, holding open the door leading to the roof. But when he found them, they were standing at the roof access door, Sam studying the door mechanism.

"Is it locked?" Shaun asked.

Sam pulled a steel pin from the handle. "No, I'm trying to figure out how to open it without setting off the alarm."

Toby turned to Shaun. "Yeah, this door is for emergencies only."

"Zombies coming to eat us qualifies as an emergency!" Shaun yelled.

"That's not what I meant," Toby said. "If we set off—"

"What pansy-pants means," Sam said. "Is if we set off the alarm, it will alert every zombie in town where we are."

A sickening moan echoed behind them. They all turned back to see four zombies turn the corner in the stairwell below.

Shaun's blood turned to ice. "I don't think our location is a huge secret, man."

Sam put her shoulder into the door and it flew open. An alarm as loud as a firehouse bell clanged. They stepped onto the roof and slammed the door behind them. Sam shoved the pin down and slipped her golf club into the locking bar. Then they all put their backs against the door.

"Is it gonna hold?" Shaun said.

Sam looked unsure. "We'll find out in a minute—"

Zombies hit the door with a thud. Sam swallowed hard and said, "—or less."

The door was holding, and the dead on the other side didn't sound happy about it. They pounded, slapped and moaned. The door shuddered but held. The three slid down into a seated position, their heavy breathing barely audible over the alarm.

"I think we're safe," Sam said.

"Don't say things like that," Shaun said.

Sam turned to him. "Like what?"

Shaun glared at Sam. "Like we're safe, or that wasn't so bad, or it can't get any worse."

"Why not?" she snapped.

"Uh, guys," Toby muttered.

"Because," Shaun said, ignoring Toby. "It's like asking for trouble."

"You're nuts," Sam said. "That's just superstitious—"

"Guys!" Toby shouted.

"WHAT!" Shaun and Sam screamed in unison.

Toby pointed at the nightmare hovering before them. Three of

Dr. Romero's giant bees, hung in the night sky above them.

"You see," Shaun said, jabbing Sam with a finger. "This is your fault."

"Oh, man." Toby's voice trembled. "Three stingers, no waiting."

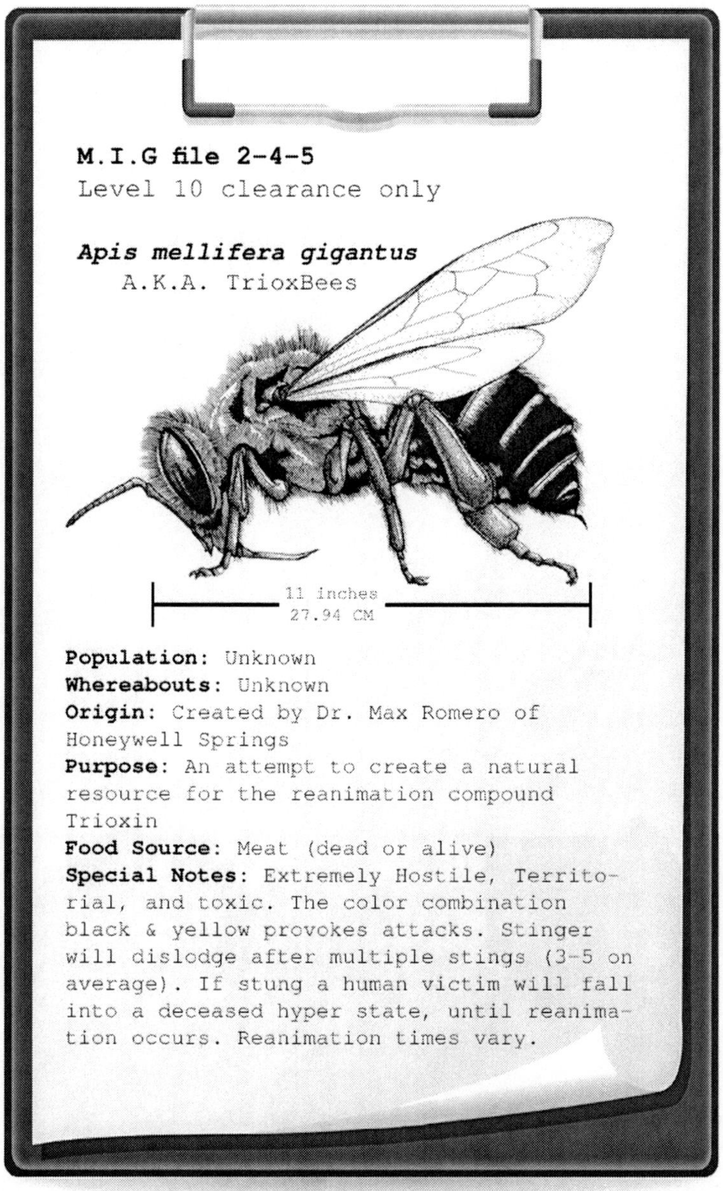

CHAPTER 12

HIGH TIME TO KILL

"Now what?" Toby said.

The three monstrous bees hovered ten feet off the ground like creepy chandeliers, ready to dive, their stingers, crimson daggers, glistening in the evening starlight.

"Okay," Shaun said, trying to stay calm, even though he could feel his lungs tightening. "On the count of three, we scatter."

Sam and Toby nodded, keeping their gaze locked on the bees.

Shaun took a deep breath, forcing his lungs open. "One..." Shaun began. "Two—" Sam and Toby jumped up and darted away in different directions. Even Sam with her injured leg moved incredibly fast, leaving Shaun, still sitting, to stare down the three monster bees. "Very nice!" Shaun said. "You guys suck!"

Shaun expected the nightmare insects to come at him. But they didn't. Instead they took off in pursuit of Sam and Toby, like dogs chasing cars. As Shaun got to his feet, he realized why. "Oh, man," he murmured to himself. "They're dead meat."

He snatched the tennis racquet and took off in the direction Toby had gone. A second later he saw Toby dive, James Bond-style, over an air conditioning unit. Two of the bees sped past him, turned around and began searching.

Running, Shaun yelled, "Take off the sweater!"

Toby rose to his knees. "What?"

"The sweater. Take off that stupid sweater!"

Toby pulled it over his head, arms raised high, just as one of the bees found him. It dived without hesitation, its stinger hitting its target like a well-thrown spear. But the bee hit the empty section of Toby's black-and-yellow sweater just over his head. With the barbs on the stinger momentarily hung up in the knitting, Shaun rushed forward, grabbed the sweater by the sleeves, and yanked it off Toby, bee and all.

It landed at Shaun's feet, the bee entangled like a fish in a net. Shaun kicked one end of the sweater, folding it over the fluttering monster insect, then jumped, bringing both feet down on the thrashing garment. There was a crunch, like stepping on popcorn. Green ooze leaked through the sweater's material.

"Shaun, look out!" Toby yelled.

Shaun looked up and swung the tennis racquet at the attacking bee. He clipped it as it swooped overhead. It spun like a piñata, about ready to burst. Before the bee regained control over its flight path, Shaun jumped up and hit it again. If it had been a piñata, candy-bee guts would have exploded all over the roof. He cut the insect in two. Each half fell to the roof. Toby stepped on the squirming half that had the head and hairy thorax as Shaun smashed its abdomen and stinger with the racquet.

Even though the bee was good and dead, Shaun wanted to keep smashing it. He wanted to beat the deadly flying menace that tried to hurt his friend until each piece was small enough to be picked up in the wind. He raised the racquet again, but just before he brought it down, Sam screamed.

The two boys took off at full speed toward the shouting. They rounded some piping and a water tank, skidding on the loose gravel that covered the roof. The rooftop was dark but Sam's screams were like a beacon. Jumping over more pipes, Shaun hit the ground a few feet from where Sam lay sprawled on her back, squirming in the gravel.

She held her arms straight out, elbows locked, and in each of her hands gripped one of the bee's wings. She must have caught it as it dived at her, and now she was stuck, unable to let go without it attacking.

Sam's panicked gaze met Shaun's. "What should I do?!"

"Don't let go," Shaun said.

"Gee, thanks. I hadn't figured that out!"

Shaun thought for a moment, gripping the racquet. If he took a swing, he would hit the bee, but probably whack Sam's hands as well. Yet a broken finger or hand was better than being dead.

"I got this," Toby said, moving toward Sam, golf club in hand.

"What're you gonna do?" Shaun said.

Toby pointed behind Shaun. "Go that way a bit, dude, and when I hit it your way, finish it off."

Shaun backed up as Toby took a stance over Sam's head. Even ten feet away, Shaun could see the fear and uncertainty on Sam's face.

"What're ya doing, dweeb?" she said, her voice shaking.

"I'm teeing off," Toby said. "Hold very still."

Toby raised the club to his shoulder. The space between Sam's hands couldn't have been more than six inches, of buzzing, angry, mutant bee. If Toby misjudged even a little…

"Fore!" Toby swung. The club sliced through the air with a swoosh. The bee rocketed forward as Toby followed through. Sam's hands still held pieces of the giant wings, but the bee itself tumbled in the air toward Shaun. Running backward and raising the tennis racquet, Shaun locked his gaze on the insect. As it came down he swung, hitting it and driving it straight into the roof.

Even wingless, stunned and broken the bee started to right itself. Shaun felt a rush of rage. He took a deep breath as he ran at the insect, racquet raised. He brought the racquet down on its head, screaming. "I hate you!"

Shaun smashed the racquet down over and over yelling, "I hate, you, I hate you, I hate you." His heart beat like a race horse, and his hands and arms began to hurt from the constant impact. But he didn't care. He wanted to pound this bee into oblivion. And not just this bee. In his mind he was pulverizing every bee that had ever terrorized him.

When exhaustion finally took hold, he stopped swinging. The racquet was just a shattered husk of twisted aluminum and broken string, and the bee, a dark green spot glistening in the gravel.

Shaun felt Toby's hand on his shoulder. "I think you got him, dude." Shaun took a painful breath, and instinctively reached for his inhaler. But before he got it out of his pocket he realized he didn't need it.

Sam hobbled over to the boys, broken wings still clutched in her fingers. Toby and Sam looked at Shaun for a few awkward moments. While smashing the bee into a green stain, he must have looked and sounded insane. *Totally cray cray.*

Sam grinned. "Did you know that killing a bee in Honeywell Springs is against the law?"

Toby abruptly started to laugh. Sam laughed too, and a second later, infected by the craziness of what had just happened, Shaun joined in.

The weight of their laughter and their shaking limbs caused the three to slump to the ground, still laughing. They laughed so hard they scarcely noticed that the alarm had cut off, and the pounding at the roof's door had stopped. After a few minutes their laughter subsided to exhausted chuckles.

Shaun studied Sam. "The bees went after you and Toby because of what you're wearing." He pointed at her black shirt. "You need to take that off. There might be more of them."

Sam looked down, then pulled the collar away from her chest, eyeing what was underneath. She let go and shook her head. "No way."

Shaun smirked. "Its nothing we haven't seen before. Well, like on the internet and stuff."

"I'm not taking off my shirt," Sam said.

"It's better than getting stung," Toby said, then held up a hand like a Boy Scout taking a pledge. "I promise we won't stare. Very much."

Sam rolled her eyes and looked under her black t-shirt again. She sighed deeply, looking unsure. "Tell you what," Sam said, looking at Shaun. "I'll take off my shirt if you tell me what your issue is with bees."

Shaun folded his arms across his chest. "I don't have an issue."

Sam tilted her head and pointed at the pile of green-and-black mush peppered with tennis racquet strings. "Seriously, inhaler-boy."

"He just doesn't like to talk about it," Toby said.

"Talk about what?" Sam said, insistently.

Toby looked at Shaun, as if asking permission to tell the story.

"Fine," Shaun said.

"When we were eight," Toby began, "our third grade class went on a fieldtrip to Tapert Farms to learn about bee-keeping. When it was over, we all got back on the bus, except Shaun here. What did you go back for again?"

"My camera," Shaun said, wanting desperately to cover his ears so he didn't have to listen. Every word that came out of Toby's mouth brought him closer to the worst moment in his life.

"Oh, yeah." Toby snapped his fingers. "So Shaun goes back—"

"Hey, wait," Sam interrupted. "I think I heard this story. It happened before I moved to Honeywell Springs, so I wasn't sure if it was true or not."

"It's true," Toby said.

"Oh, man," Sam said. "That was you?"

Shaun nodded and pulled his knees to his chest. "I wasn't looking where I was going and I tripped. I fell through several honeycomb hives and into a ditch. The framed boxes with all the bees fell in with me. They started stinging me." Shaun took a deep breath and closed his eyes, picturing the horrible scene, bees swarming, crawling all over him. "I'd been stung before, so the first few didn't bother me too bad, but when I realized I couldn't get out of the ditch, I started…" Shaun shook his head, trying to erase the images, then opened his eyes. "They say I passed out after the first few hundred stings. I woke up in the hospital nine days later."

Toby put a hand on Shaun's back. "No one even knew he was gone until the bus driver did a head count. He must have been down there a half hour."

"How many times did you get stung?" Sam asked.

"Oh, that's the worst part," Toby said. "He missed the world record by just one sting." Toby held up a finger. "One."

"Yeah that was the worst part." Shaun rolled his eyes. "Not the nearly dying part, or the months in recovery, or my new asthma problem, or the panic attacks, the nightmares—not to mention the last five years of therapy."

"Hey, I'm just saying," Toby said, "if you have to get stung that many times, you might as well get the record, man. Some dude in Zimbabwe holds the record with 2,443 stings, and Shaun missed it by—"

"One," Shaun snapped. "She heard you the first time."

"Okay," Toby said, shrinking a little.

Sam's forehead furrowed. "So if this thing that happened caused your issue with bees, why stay in Honeywell Springs, the honey bee capital of the world. Why didn't your family just move?"

"Really?" Toby snickered. "Don't you know who Shaun's family is?"

"Should I?" Sam said.

"My last name is Ripley," Shaun said.

"Ripley," Sam repeated. "Of Ripley's Honey?"

Toby nodded. "That's the one."

"My family has owned the largest factory here since before the town even had a name. My mom wanted to move, but my dad disagreed." Shaun deepened his voice, imitating his father. "No son of mine is going to be afraid of bees. Shaun will live in Honeywell Springs and face his fears like a man."

"If you don't mind me saying, bro," Toby said, "your dad is kind of a jerk."

Shaun wanted to be mad at Toby for slamming his dad, but he couldn't. Fact was none of that mattered anymore. All that did matter was for the three of them to stay alive.

"Okay," Shaun said, turning his attention to Sam. "Off with it."

Sam acted like she didn't know what he was talking about.

"Come on," Shaun said. "There could be more of them around and I don't want Toby or me to have to risk our lives to save you, just because you decided to keep wearing a black shirt.

Sam sighed. "Okay, but don't…"

"Don't what?" Toby said.

"Oh, the heck with it." Sam quickly slipped the black t-shirt over her head.

Shaun and Toby sat motionless for a few beats, staring at Sam, neither of them able to comprehend what they were looking at. When it finally sunk in, Shaun's mouth fell open.

"O.M.…" Shaun was way too shocked to finish with a G.

CHAPTER

13

SKYFALL

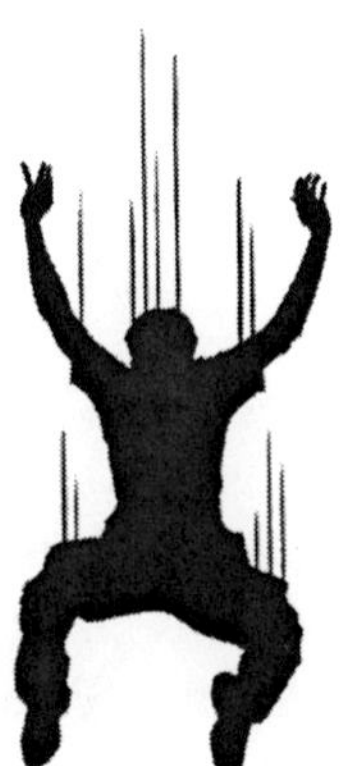

"Wow," Shaun said.

"Yeah," Toby managed. "What he said."

Sam folded her arms over her chest, but it did very little to hide the fluorescent pink, rainbow and butterfly covered, Hello Kitty t-shirt that somehow found its way onto tough-girl, motorcycle daredevil, Sam Campbell.

Shaun stared, not even trying to hide his confusion. It was like seeing the Hulk in a tutu, or Batman wearing pastel colors. It was just wrong. So very wrong.

"It was a gift from my dad," Sam said, her cheeks turning crimson.

"I like it," Toby said. "It brings out the color in your hair."

Shaun looked at Toby as if he'd lost his mind. Toby shrugged, and Shaun looked back at Sam. For an instant the bully who had poured dirt down his shirt and relentlessly called Toby names like pansy pants, disappeared. Shaun saw wavy red curls, deep green eyes, flush cheeks, and soft lips. And just for a moment he saw not Sam, but Samantha. A girl. One that was almost pretty.

Sam dropped her black No Fear t-shirt, turned from the boys and walked away. The sight of her limping reminded Shaun of the ice he'd snagged. He scooped up the shirt and told Toby to stay with Sam. He then retrieved the ice trays, dumped the ice into the shirt and went looking for his fellow zombie apocalypse survivors.

He found Sam and Toby leaning on the safety wall overlooking Main Street. Shaun wrapped the shirt, filled with ice, around Sam's knee.

Sam seemed to barely notice that Shaun was doing this, but suddenly looked and nodded. "That feels good. Thanks," she said softly.

Shaun joined them and gazed down into town. Zombies filled the street below. From this height, and because of the bouncing antennas most wore, they looked like ants. One of the VIP's corpses was half in, half out of one of the limos. A zombie in a bright yellow shirt with a black vest sunk its teeth into an ankle and tore off the foot.

Toby turned away and Shaun looked at him, surprised. "I thought you liked horror."

Toby shook his head. "Not this much horror. If we get out of this, I'm done with zombie movies."

"What do you think they're doing?" Sam said.

Toby peered back down. "Looking for food, maybe."

"Yes, but it's the way they're looking," Sam said. "In zombie movies all the walking dead just shamble around aimlessly. But these ones kind of move in lines, following one another."

Sam's right. And the way they followed each other was yet another way they looked like ants. Ants at a picnic. Shaun followed the staggering lines of black-and-yellow zombies. Pointing at the building next door he said, "They all seem to be going or coming out of the Honeywell Community Theater."

"Maybe they're having a meeting?" Sam said.

Shaun could see through the windows into the huge auditorium. His family had donated most of the money to build the theater and he could remember his dad saying it was state-of-the-art, quite large for a community the size of Honeywell Springs. If filled to capacity, it could seat more than half the town. Maybe even the whole town if everyone stood and scrunched together.

Something crashed into a theater window from the inside. It was one of Dr. Romero's Bees, its grotesque stinger scraping the window like a knife on a chalkboard.

"Okay, I've seen enough," Shaun said. "We need to get out of here."

"Off the roof?" Toby said.

"Off the roof, away from this store and out of Honeywell Springs," Shaun said. "If we don't, we're as good as zom*bee* food. And I don't know about you guys, but that's not the way I want to check out."

"Okay," Toby said, looking into the street. "Those things are everywhere. What's your plan?"

Shaun grinned. "What would 007 do?"

Toby smirked. "Call MI-6 and have a helicopter pick him up."

Shaun shook his head. "He only calls for a pickup at the end of the movie."

Toby snapped his fingers. "Unless he wants to spend some one-on-one time with the hot spy lady he rescues."

"Oh, yeah," Shaun said.

"Will you dweebs stop talking nerd," Sam said.

"Sorry," Shaun said. "The point is that James Bond would find a way out of this situation, and that's what we need to do—come up with a plan."

Sam folded her arms. "Will it be a stupid plan, like walking on the heads of zombies?"

"Hey," Toby said. "That actually worked."

Shaun nodded. "I can't lie, whatever escape plan we come up with, stupidity may be involved."

Sam sighed, flashing a look of surrender. "All right, I'm in. I've stuck with you guys this far. Might as well stick it out to see how we all die."

"That's the spirit," Shaun said. "Sort of."

"I'm with you as always, dude." Toby bumped fist with him. "It's 007 time."

The plan was probably not James Bond-worthy, but then again 007 never faced a zombie apocalypse.

"Okay, let me just recap this plan of yours," Sam said looking over the edge of the department store building, down into the alley where they had left the golf cart. "You want us to climb down the escape ladder on the backside of the building."

"Only as far as the new storage facility," Shaun said. "We jump off onto its roof, then head over there to the wall at the end of the alley. We jump down into the alley, run to the golf cart, load up, and blow this taco stand."

The alley they had almost gotten trapped in was zombie-free for the moment. The dead had either staggered back to Main Street or were inside the department store, still hunting for them. The dumpster that had saved Toby's life, with its wheels no longer locked, had rolled to the end of the alley and was resting against the wall. Facing the wrong direction, the golf cart was about fifteen feet away and looked to be in good shape.

Sam pointed at the storage building's wall. "It's twenty feet, maybe more."

"It'll be like falling from the sky," Toby said.

"Yeah," Shaun said. "Not a fun drop, I know, but if you aim for the dumpster, there're some good-sized garbage bags to land on."

"Make sure you land in the front of the dumpster," Toby added. "The back is filled with sharp hunks of metal."

"Wonderful," Sam said. "You did say the plan might be stupid."

"What's stupider is waiting up here for more giant bees to find us," Shaun said.

Sam and Toby agreed, then they all headed for the escape ladder on the backside of the building. A year ago they would have been able to use it to go all the way to street level, but the new storage building was so close to the department store, the ladder had to be cut short, leaving those escaping a fire stranded on the new roof.

They made it down the ladder, no problem. With her wounded knee, Sam had to take the rungs one at a time, keeping most of her weight on her good leg, but she kept pace with the boys. They moved quietly to the wall that dropped into the alley and peered down.

"Who's going first?" Toby said.

Shaun looked at Toby, holding up his fist. "Throw for it."

Toby smiled and held up his fist.

"What're you dweebs doing?" Sam said.

"Rock, Paper, Scissors, Lizard, Spock, to see who goes first," Shaun said.

"It's like Rock, Paper, Scissors," Toby added, "But with two more—"

"My God, you guys are dorks." Without another word, Sam vaulted over the building's edge.

Shaun and Toby were so stunned they just stared at one another until they heard the metallic thud below. They rushed to the edge and peered down. The alley wasn't lit, and the dumpster was dark inside. Shaun held his breath waiting to see movement, some sign that Sam had made it and wasn't lying at the bottom of the trash bin with a broken neck.

A hand shot up from the darkness, reaching for the dumpster's edge. Sam's head, topped with red curls and trash, rose from the shadows. She stood, looked up, and grinned. "That was awesome!"

Figures she'd enjoy that. For a daredevil like Sam, dropping twenty feet into a dumpster was probably something she had on her to-do list anyway.

"Well," Toby said, "see you at the bottom." He dangled his legs over the edge and dropped.

Shaun watched him fall and caught Sam's expression as she realized Toby was coming straight at her. She dove to the other side of the bin as Toby landed with a loud thud. Shaun could hear Sam yelling and Toby apologizing. But Shaun wasn't the only one listening to the commotion. At the Main Street end, several zombies were turning their undead attention into the alley.

"Guys! Be quiet!" Realizing he had just yelled louder than either of Sam and Toby, Shaun slapped himself on the forehead. *Idiot!*

As zombies entered the alley, Shaun threw his legs over the edge. Sam and Toby had already exited the dumpster and were heading toward the cart. Hopefully by the time he got there they'd have it turned around and ready for him to jump in.

Shaun stared down into the dumpster, a black bottomless rectangle. He tried to take a deep breath but his lungs began to tighten. If he waited much longer, breathing would become difficult, and he would end up lying down on this roof and never get up. He held his breath, took aim, and jumped.

The darkness rushed toward him as he fell. Halfway down he sensed his aim was off, but he couldn't change the angle of his descent. He hit the bin just off-center. His landing knocked the air out of him. He needed to bounce up and get moving, but his knees had come down on the metal in the back of the dumpster. Were they bleeding? He tried to breathe but his lungs felt heavy, inflexible, like stone.

He wanted to reach for his inhaler but he lay crumpled in a ball surrounded by garbage and darkness. *No, I'm not dying here.* With all his might he inhaled deeply, forcing his lungs to breathe. He took in the awful stench of old lunch leftovers, dirty socks, and whatever else was around him, but it was air.

"Shaun, come on!" Toby screamed.

"Get a move on, dweeb," Sam said.

Shaun rose out of the dumpster like a whale breaching the ocean's surface. He bounded out and ran to the cart. Sam was driving, swinging it around, tires spinning on the alley floor. Shaun leaped onto the back of the cart as a dozen zombies migrated down the alley.

"Hold on," Sam said. "This is going to be bumpy!"

The cart accelerated. Sam was going to drive straight through them. She swerved the cart, trying to avoid the dead but they were everywhere. The first collision was only a slight jostle. A man in an extravagant bee costume spun full circle, then careened into the alley wall. The next collision rocketed the cart up as it rolled over someone. Shaun nearly bounced out. He was about to complain about their reckless speed, but they were only a few yards from Main Street, and the last thing he wanted Sam to do was slow down.

Just one turn, he thought, *and we're on Main Street, then out of town.*

But before Sam turned onto Main Street and freedom, an undead man with a familiar face lurched in front of the cart.

It was Mr. Hooper, looking as disapproving as ever.

The cart hit the mountain of a man, and Shaun held on tight as their escape vehicle began to tip over.

CHAPTER

14

MIDSUMMER'S NIGHT DOOM

For an instant, Shaun thought the daredevil in Sam Campbell was going to successfully steer the golf cart on two wheels until it somehow righted itself. But she over-corrected, jerking the cart in the wrong direction. It tipped over, slamming down on Toby's side with a horrific crash. Sparks flew in the night air as they slid ten feet across the asphalt. The cart came to rest against the curb with a smack.

When Shaun finally opened his eyes he was lying on his side, his cheek against the cold street. All he could see was the topsy turvy cart, and dead feet shuffling his way.

"Abandon ship!" Toby yelled.

"They're everywhere," Sam screamed.

Looking panicked, Toby and Sam helped Shaun to his feet. They were surrounded by bouncing black-and-yellow antennas, broken wings, and undead eyes staring at them, hungry.

"What now?" Toby said.

"Uh..." That was all Shaun could manage as the people of Honeywell Springs—people he had known all his life—closed in like circling sharks before a feeding frenzy.

"Hey, do you hear it?" Sam said. "The limos. We need to get to a limo."

Sam grabbed a new golf club from the bag on the cart, then pushed Shaun forward, toward the zombies.

Shaun tried to resist. "What're you doing?"

Sam stepped in front of Shaun and Toby, brandishing her club. "The chauffeurs left the limos running. We need to get in one, now." With a grunt, she swung the club and smacked Principal Rooney in the neck. The man toppled aside, opening a passage through the undead crowd.

"That'll cost me some detention." Sam looked back at the boys. "Come on, dweebs!"

With Sam leading the way, they fought their way to the nearest limo, about ten yards away.

Toby joined Sam up front, swinging his club like a golf pro. His swings cut through the air, and after each one a zombie spun out of the way. Shaun glanced back. The black-and-yellow mass was closing in behind them. If they were going to make it to the limo, they needed to slow their pursuers down. But he didn't have a club, and his tennis racquet was up on the roof in a pile of green bee guts. *The sling shot!*

He snatched it from his back pocket and flipped open the pack of ammo. His fingers moved so frantically that he dropped most of the pellets, but he managed to load one. Without aiming he fired point blank into the zombies behind them. There was a *swoosh*, then a *ping*, as his pellet smacked one of Sheriff Rosco's deputies in the forehead. The deputy dropped to his knees and to Shaun's amazement other zombies, so determined to reach Shaun, tripped over the kneeling lawman. Zombies fell over one another like characters in a cartoon.

Shaun would have laughed if he wasn't so unbelievably terrified.

"Come on, Shaun," Toby yelled.

Shaun turned around. Toby was sitting in the back compartment of a limo, motioning him inside. Shaun leaped forward like a football player diving across the goal line. He landed inside and Toby shut the door. Shaun tried to sit up, but the limo suddenly accelerated, and he slid across the floor. The passenger compartment was almost as big as Shaun's bedroom, and he rolled several feet before coming to a stop under a cocktail table. He tried to sit up again, but smacked his head on the table's underside.

The whole world spun to the left, then abruptly whirled to the right. From outside there was thud after thud as the limo bumped into zombies.

Toby fell on the floor landing next to Shaun.

"Who the heck is driving?" Shaun screamed.

"Who do you think?" Toby shouted.

Shaun was about to try and sit up again when he noticed, dangling over the seat above him, a twitching hand missing two fingers. Shaun crawled away as fast as he could. Toby sat up as he moved by, then immediately crawled after him.

After they'd scurried away as far as they could, they turned around. A plump woman wearing a polo shirt embroidered with the Thrift-Mart logo sat up. Her hair was in disarray, her right foot missing along with several patches of skin, as if she'd been gnawed on. She brought her foot and stump down on Toby's golf club and Shaun's sling shot. In their panic they'd left their weapons behind.

"Oh, man," Toby said. "It's one of the VIPs, dude. She's infected."

"Ya' think?" Shaun pounded on the glass separating them from the driver. "Saaaam!"

Sam hit a button on the dash, lowering the glass. "Hey, I'm kind of busy up here," she said over her shoulder.

"Well, we sort of have a little problem back here!" Shaun said. The woman took a gimpy step, hunching forward like some deformed creature.

"Can't you guys just deal—" Sam eyes went wide in the rearview mirror. "Hey, there's a zombie back there with you!"

"Yeah, thanks for that status update," Shaun said. "Now stop the car and let us out!"

"I can't, there's too many out there," Sam said. "But I got an idea. I'll slow down, you open a door, then you two grab hold of something."

"I really hate the sound of that plan," Shaun said.

"Trust me," Sam said.

Shaun looked at Toby, who shrugged.

"I don't think we have much choice." Toby reached over and grabbed a door handle. He flung the door wide, then the boys dove under the cocktail table and grasped a leg.

The limo whipped to the right. The zombie tumbled to the side of the compartment opposite the open door. Sam spun the limo violently the other way, and the zombie rolled like a massive snowball to the other side and bounced out the open door. The limo continued sliding until it jolted to a stop.

"Well, don't just lie there, you idiots," Sam yelled. "Shut the door!"

Toby crawled to the door and pulled it closed. A second later Sam hit the gas and they were off again.

With the image of the VIP zombie fresh in Shaun's mind, he wasn't interested in riding in the huge passenger compartment. He could still see the thing staggering toward them, teeth snapping, bloody hands outstretched. Shaun and Toby took turns climbing through the glass opening to the driver's compartment, each of them flopping hard onto the front bench seat.

Sam bounced as each one hit the wide leather seat. She glowered at them then suddenly snapped forward and hit the brakes. Not having seatbelts on Shaun and Toby slid off the seat and smacked into the dashboard. They sat up slowly. A box truck was parked at the end of the carnival area, and its back end stuck out into the street. A large industrial dolly and several boxes of honeydogs lay scattered on the asphalt like a child's building blocks.

"Sorry about that, guys," Sam said.

"That's okay," Toby said. "It's been kind of a slam-your-head-into-a-dashboard sort of night."

Shaun gazed out the windshield. They were near the end of Main Street. A few black and yellow streamers decorated the street lights and buildings, but the bulk of the Founder's Day Festival was behind them.

Sam threw the limo into park. "Where to now?"

Shaun hadn't given much thought to where they should go when they made it out of town. Truth was, he wasn't certain they'd make it this far. "I don't think this is happening everywhere," Shaun said.

"How do you figure?" Sam said.

"Do the math," Shaun said. "There were only six hundred and sixty-seven infected bees to start with, and according to Dr. Romero they could only sting four or five times before kicking the bucket. It looked to me as if they stung everyone in Honeywell Springs except us. That would pretty much take most of the bee's stingers to do that."

"We did find a few flying around," Sam said. "Remember?"

How could I forget? The image of a giant bee diving at his head was one that would surely be popping up in future nightmares. "I know, but for some reason they stayed here."

"So all we need to do is head to the closest town and find some help," Toby said.

"Harpers Eve is about twelve miles away," Sam said. "Got some cousins there."

"What if you're wrong and the bees are already there?" Toby asked.

"Cross that bridge when we come to it, I guess," Shaun said.

Sam took a deep breath, then put the limo into drive. As she steered around the dolly in the street, Shaun turned and looked behind them. A hundred yards back coming from the festival area, a black-and-yellow mass of zombies shambled after them.

He couldn't see their faces but he knew they were the people he had grown up with: friends, neighbors, relatives, and even the bullies. He felt uneasy leaving them all behind. Even though they had tried to eat him, they were family and Honeywell Springs was home.

Shaun and Toby had gathered inspiration from their hero, 007, to escape a horrible zombie death, and Shaun should be happy that they had, or at least relieved. But as he watched the townsfolk of Honeywell Springs fall away into the distance, it didn't feel like the end of a James Bond movie. This was not a happy ending. Not even a little bit.

They rode in silence for the last two miles out of town. The silhouettes of houses melted into the countryside, scarcely illuminated in the moonless sky. He wondered what they'd say to the sheriff in Harpers Eve. *Will he even believe us?*

The limo's headlights lit up the familiar city limits sign, and Shaun read it for what he assumed would be the last time. Then the road ahead suddenly became ablaze with light.

Sam slammed on the brakes, and the boys hit the dashboard, again. Shaun and Toby pushed themselves up and gazed out at what seemed like every spotlight in the county, all aimed at them. Shaun shielded his eyes from the light, and could make out the shadowy shapes of men with rifles standing on what had to be tanks.

"Oh, thank God," Toby said. "The cavalry is here."

Sam put the limo into park. "About frickin' time."

"You think they're here to rescue us?" Shaun said.

"What else?" Sam said.

Before Shaun could answer, a voice boomed over a megaphone from outside. "You have thirty seconds to exit the vehicle, or you will be fired upon."

"That doesn't sound very *rescuey*," Toby said.

"So not," Sam agreed.

Shaun swallowed hard. "What should we—"

"You now have twenty seconds!"

Sam threw the door open, and they all slid out on the driver's side as fast as they could. The boys took position on either side of her, standing close enough to touch shoulders. Even though the night air was warm, Shaun felt chilled. He could feel Sam shaking.

"Advance and be recognized," the voice ordered.

"What does that mean?" Toby said.

"I don't know." Shaun shrugged. "Step forward and say hello, maybe."

The three of them stepped forward two paces, stopped, then all said, "Hello."

"State your name!"

Shaun stepped forward. "I'm Ripley, Shaun Ripley. This is Samantha Campbell, and that's Toby Parker."

"Have you been stung?"

Shaun's fear was beginning to melt away, and exhaustion was taking its place. "Look, we've had a really awful night, can you—"

"Shut up and answer the question," snapped the disembodied voice behind the beams of light.

"How can I shut up *and* answer the question?" Shaun fired back.

There was a pause, then the voice returned a little less harsh. "Sorry, son. It's been a long night for everybody. Now please, just answer the question. Have any of you been stung?"

"No," Shaun said, folding his arms.

"Has anyone been bitten?"

"No."

"Are any of you undead?"

"Seriously?"

"All right, hold your position."

There was a popping sound, as if the megaphone had been switched off. Shaun looked at his companions, each mirrored his own confusion.

"Okay, Shaun, Samantha, and Todd," the voice began again.

"His name is Toby," Shaun said.

"Yes, yes, Toby. For now we need you three to disrobe."

"Disrobe!" Shaun said. "You mean like take our clothes off?"

"Affirmative."

The three exchanged glances.

"What is wrong with these people?" Sam said softly.

Shaun raised his hand like a student wanting a teacher's attention. "Uh, excuse me. Is there possibly anybody else back there we could talk to?"

CHAPTER 15

BLAST FROM THE PAST

While they stripped down to their underwear, Sam made Toby and Shaun stand in front with their backs to her. They threw their clothes and shoes in a pile as instructed, then with hands raised walked forward. Shaun went first, with Toby close behind, then Sam.

A few of the spotlights dimmed as they neared a corridor of soldiers. Rifles were pointed at them as they walked between two tanks, then toward more soldiers and what looked like a hastily assembled campsite right on the road. It had sandbag bunkers, army trucks, even a lookout tower with a serious looking cannon up top.

A solider holding a megaphone stepped in front of Shaun. The lights were softer in the campsite, and the man didn't look as fierce as his voice had been over the megaphone. He seemed sincere but cautious. He motioned for them to stop. "Are any of you hurt?"

Shaun felt a flash of anger. He had already answered this guy's questions and stripped almost naked at gunpoint. He didn't know what to expect after escaping Honeywell Springs, but this definitely wasn't it.

"I told you, we're not stung or bitten," Shaun said.

The man motioned for them to lower their hands. "I mean, any other kind of injuries. Twisted ankles, scrapes, bruises."

Shaun lowered his hands. "Sam—Samantha—hurt her knee. She smashed it in a golf cart crash."

"And you hit her with that engine part," Toby added.

"Yeah, and, I sort of hit her with an engine part." Shaun sighed. "Thanks, Toby."

"I'm here to help, bro."

The man in fatigues glanced back at Sam. "Okay, let's get you guys through decontamination. Then we'll see to Miss Campbell's leg."

Shaun turned around to check on his friends, but instantly became distracted by Sam, or more importantly, Samantha's sports bra. He was about to look away when flames exploded a dozen yards behind Sam.

A soldier wearing a gas mask was igniting their pile of clothes with a flame thrower.

The three entered a decontamination chamber the size of a walk-in closet. It looked like some futuristic stand-up Jacuzzi. Once inside they separated, Sam on one side, Toby and Shaun on the other, their backs facing the center. Shaun and Toby did their best not to look at Sam, but even Shaun found it strangely difficult.

Toby leaned over and whispered in Shaun's ear. "Is Sam wearing boxers?"

"I don't know," Shaun whispered back. "Didn't get a good look."

"You want to take a peek?" Toby suggested.

"Not me. You peek."

"No, you."

"You."

"If either of you dweebs turn around, I'll beat the stupid out of both of you," Sam said.

Shaun closed his eyes. "I don't think we should peek."

"Good call, dude."

A mist filled the room from all sides. It tingled. Shaun imagined they were being dipped in an enormous vat of 7UP. The sensation lasted a few minutes, then the sound of a vacuum filled the chamber. In the blink of an eye, the mist was gone. Lights flashed green above them, and a computerized voice said, "Decontamination complete."

With a mechanical whine, the chamber door opened on the opposite side from where they'd entered. Shaun and Toby stood still a moment, awaiting instruction. After a minute, Shaun glanced around the chamber. Sam was gone.

Shaun nudged Toby and they both stepped through the open door. They met the soldier they spoke to earlier. He had ditched the megaphone and now held two gray jumpsuits, socks, and Velcro-strap shoes, all made from the same material. He tossed them to the boys.

Shaun caught his. "Where's Sam?"

"She's on her way to the infirmary. They'll check her out and take care of her knee."

Shaun felt relieved. He stepped into his jumpsuit. It was a pretty good fit, and the areas that were loose were easily tightened with a series of chrome zippers. The jumpsuit wasn't orange, or white with black stripes like he'd seen inmates wear in prison movies, but Shaun wondered if they were in some kind of jail.

The solider led them to a huge military vehicle. It looked like a mobile city, with different compartments. Shaun couldn't tell how many because they were ushered along too fast. They hurried past a lab, an armory, and then into a small room with a metal table, uncomfortable looking chairs and an analog clock hung high on the wall. It was almost 2:00 a.m.

The soldier didn't follow them inside. The big man grabbed the door handle. "Take a seat, guys," he said. "They'll be in to debrief you in a minute."

Shaun asked, "Who will be in to debrief us?" But his words bounded off the closing metal door, which snapped shut with an ominous *clunk*.

Shaun sighed. "This night doesn't seem to be getting better, does it?"

"At least no one is trying to eat us," Toby said.

We just got here, Shaun thought. *Give it an hour or two.*

Toby walked over to the far wall, which was covered with a huge mirror. Shaun had seen enough cop shows to know there were eyes on the other side of that glass, watching.

Toby tapped the mirror, then waved into it. "You think we're under arrest," he said over his shoulder.

"I don't think these are the kind of people who go around arresting," Shaun said.

Toby turned around. "What kind of people are they?"

Before Shaun could answer, the door swung open. Two men dressed in identical charcoal-gray suits and thin black ties stepped in. The taller of the two looked at Toby. "To answer your question, Son, good people," he said. He then smiled, flashing immaculately white teeth. They looked so perfect it seemed he'd never chewed anything in his life. "Everything is going to be okay."

The shorter one stepped close to Shaun, displaying an equally perfect smile. "Why don't you boys take a seat, and we'll get started."

Shaun and Toby sat in the chairs, which were even more uncomfortable than they looked. The two men sat opposite them. Shaun wasn't sure if their grins were supposed to put them at ease or terrify them. Shaun went with *terrify*.

"I'm Major Captain," the taller man said, then motioned to his associate. "And this is Captain Major. We're part of a special unit, M.I.G. Sometimes referred to as the Men In Gray.

Shaun said, "You mean, like Men In Black?"

Major Captain scoffed. "Yes and no. M.I.B. deals with alien and extraterrestrial incursions."

Toby asked, "Aliens *and* extraterrestrials? What's the difference?"

"That's classified, Son," Captain Major said. "We at M.I.G. deal exclusively with zombie uprisings."

Shaun and Toby looked back, uncertain.

"You know," Captain Major continued. "The undead, flesh-eaters, zuvembie, the living dead, rot-walkers, skin-puppets, brain-munchers, the walking dead, meat bags—"

"Captain," Major Captain said. "I think they get the idea."

"There are enough zombie uprisings to have a government unit?" Toby asked.

Major Captain flashed a knowing smile. "More than you might think, and I never said we were with the government."

Captain Major pulled out an inhaler, expensive looking, and a box of albuterol. He slid them across the table toward Shaun. "I believe yours was incinerated."

"Yeah, it was," Shaun said. "Along with all our clothes. Was that really necessary?"

"Standard M.I.G. containment protocol," Major Captain said. "Since the first zombie uprising in 1968, the elite members of M.I.G. have kept the public safe with a strict adherence to its protocols. Any deviation puts all of humanity at risk."

Shaun picked up the box of albuterol. His name was scrawled across the label. "How did you even know I needed this?"

Captain Major opened a file folder that matched the color of the table so much, Shaun didn't notice it until it was flipped open. Captain Major lifted a paper and began to read. "Shaun Felix Ripley, age thirteen, born to Phyllis and William Ripley. Employed at Honeywell Market, job performance marginal, grades average, plays far too many video games, does not play sports—"

"Hey," Shaun said. "I play soccer."

"Oh, I'm sorry," Captain Major said, pointing into the file. "It says, should *not* play sports."

Toby chuckled at Shaun. "True story, dude."

Shaun sighed. "Shut up."

"When you were eight," Captain Major continued, "you were stung an incredible amount of times, missing the world record for a bee sting survivor by just one. Last year you had a crush on Alice Honeychile, but failed to—"

"Okay, I get it," Shaun said. "You know a lot about me."

"Oh, do me," Toby said. "What does it say in there about me?"

Major Captain flashed irritation, but Captain Major reached in the file and pulled out another paper. "Toby Stanly Parker, also age thirteen, born to Richard and Mary Parker, never employed, slightly less video gaming than Shaun, average grades, plays golf with a…" Captain Major paused, as if he needed to take a second look at what he'd read. "A nine handicap." He looked at Toby. "Nice."

"Thanks. I play—"

"Gentlemen," Major Captain said. "We aren't here to chit-chat. This is a debriefing. Let's get started."

"Yes, of course," Captain Major said, sliding some photos from under the file. He spread them before Toby and Shaun. "These are satellite images showing you two leaving Dr. Romero's house just before the outbreak."

"Wow." Toby pulled one closer. The pictures shot from Earth's orbit had amazing detail. Toby's hideous turquoise pants stood out like a you-are-here marker on a mall map, making it easy for the boys to locate themselves. "This is so much better than Google Maps," Toby said. "Is my head really that big?"

"Yes," Shaun confirmed. "Yes it is."

"We want you to tell us everything you heard, saw, and

experienced after arriving at the doctor's place," Captain Major said.

"With particular detail about anything the doctor told you," Major Captain added.

It took nearly an hour to tell the men of M.I.G. what they wanted to know. If Shaun and Toby had been allowed to talk without interruption, the story would have taken only ten minutes, but Major Captain kept stopping them to ask questions or request that they repeat certain parts—anything to do with the doctor. It seemed they didn't trust Dr. Romero.

When they got to the part about tying Sheriff Rosco's body to a table in the doctor's lab, the men asked over and over if Shaun and Toby were positive he was dead. Every time they said yes, Captain Major and Major Captain exchanged glances, then wrote in their notebooks.

Shaun looked up at the clock. It was 3:25 a.m. He should be exhausted. He'd never been able to stay up until midnight on New Years Eve in his life, and here it was deep in the a.m., and he was totally awake, and hungry. *Near-death experiences must have the same effect as a pot of coffee.*

Shaun's stomach growled. "As fun as telling you guys the same story over and over is, can we get something to eat?"

Major Captain held up a finger and his concentration seemed to drift away. It was only then that Shaun realized that both men had tiny ear pieces in. Someone was obviously talking to Major Captain. He nodded and said, "Okay, I want our team to substantiate the findings before we make a decision." He nodded again. "I know it's outside the protocol."

Shaun looked at Toby, feeling totally ignored. Toby just shrugged.

"Out," Major Captain said, then looked at the boys. "We'll take you to the mess to get something to eat, but first some friendly faces would like to say hi."

The two M.I.G. men rose in unison, almost like synchronized robots, and exited the room without another word. Shaun and Toby sat quietly for a few beats, staring at the door.

Toby finally broke the silence. "You think Sam is okay?"

"You know Sam," Shaun said. "She'll have busted out of here by daybreak, if she's not already gone."

Toby started to laugh, when the door suddenly swung open. In walked a tall thin woman, wearing a similar charcoal-gray suit as the M.I.G. guys wore, minus the tie. She smiled at the boys and it wasn't the creepy, terrifying kind of smile. It was sweet, sincere, and downright familiar.

Shaun searched for her name. "Ellen?" he said. "Ellen Honeychile, is that you?"

She nodded. Shaun and Toby's babysitter from six or seven years ago looked as happy to see them as they were to see her. Neither of them had seen their neighbor, Alice Honeychile's older sister, since she left to attend the Air Force Academy. It had been a big deal in Honeywell Springs, her being the first student from the area accepted.

"Ellen." Surprise rose in Toby's voice.

"Well, around here, I'm Lieutenant Corporal," she said.

Shaun said, "Really?"

She nodded. "Code names. They're awful."

"Really awful," Shaun said.

"I know. There's a suggestion box, but they never listen."

Shaun wanted to vault over the table and hug his old babysitter, but before he could, Dr. Romero walked in, followed closely by Sam. They both had on gray jumpsuits, and Sam wore a brace around her knee, but she walked as if her leg was uninjured. Shaun started around the table to embrace them all, but before he got there someone else stepped in, and Shaun stopped dead in his tracks, shocked and confused.

"But you're dead," Toby said.

Wearing a gray jumpsuit, although a much larger one, Sheriff Rosco grinned at the boys. He didn't look dead, or undead, and was definitely not a zombie. He was alive!

CHAPTER 16

BLOOD FEVER

The food was cold and the soda was warm, but Shaun, Toby and Sam consumed them like they hadn't eaten in a week. They sat inside a large camouflage-colored tent, with picnic tables and a makeshift kitchen. While they ate, Dr. Romero explained how Sheriff Rosco had made the journey from corpse strapped to a lab table back to the land of the living.

"After you boys left," the doctor said, "I began working on a more potent antidote, utilizing my own blood as a catalyst. If given within the first few hours, the infection is reversible." He gestured to Sheriff Rosco who sat down at the table with a second helping of food.

"I don't remember much," Rosco said, picking up his fork. "I only recall arriving at the Doc's house and meeting that woman from animal control. Next thing I know I'm waking up in a helicopter, on our way here."

"So…" Shaun started, but had to finish swallowing first. "So, these M.I.G. people picked you up. How did they know to come get you?"

"Remember the phone call I made after calling the sheriff?" Dr. Romero said.

"The number on the tank," Toby said.

"That's the one. I thought I was calling for assistance. Turns out I was calling these guys," Dr. Romero said with disdain. "First thing M.I.G. did was cut us off from the rest of the world."

"Is that why the phones don't work?" Sam asked.

The doctor replied. "Internet, broadcast signals, WiFi, all cut off. It's part of their containment protocol." Dr. Romero leaned forward and lowered his voice. "They're not here to help us."

"Now, Doc," Rosco said. "You don't really know that."

Ellen sat down with a tray of food and Dr. Romero looked at her. "Tell them," he said. "Tell them you're not here to help us."

Shaun could tell by the look on her face that what the doctor said was true. She'd changed a lot in just a few years. She looked so plain. A far cry from the energetic teenager he had his first crush on.

Ellen forced a smile. "I assure you they are considering your proposal to save the town. Just give them some time. They've never, as far as I know, had to consider a possible cure for an undead uprising. All the protocols are designed around the Q.C.C. methodology."

"Q.C.C?" Shaun said, then took a sip of warm Sprite.

"Quarantine, Contain, and Cleanse," Dr. Romero said.

"Cleanse?" Toby said. "You mean like clean the town up."

"No," Dr. Romero said. "Obliterate, erase, make disappear."

Shaun's stomach sank.

"Settle down, Doc," Rosco said. "You're scarin' the kids. And me."

"It won't come to that," Ellen said, gesturing to Dr. Romero. "We have a cure this time. I'm sure they will come to the conclusion that Honeywell Springs doesn't need to be cleansed."

"Have they cleansed towns before?" Shaun asked, his gaze aimed at Ellen.

She nodded. "I've seen it done three times. Each time it was necessary. If just one of those plagues had got out…"

"Where?" Sam said.

Ellen ticked off the names on her fingers. "Saint Hugo in France, Stoker Cove in Ottawa, and Nebula Falls in South Dakota."

"I never heard of those towns," Sam said.

"And you never will," Dr. Romero said. "That's the point. They don't just cleanse the land, but the very memory of its existence."

Shaun was already struggling to accept that the people of Honeywell Springs might be a lost cause. Now these M.I.G. guys were going to erase everything he had ever known. The good, the bad, the very existence of Honeywell Springs. Shaun looked at Ellen. "How did you get mixed up with these guys?"

"Yeah," Toby added. "No one has heard much from you since you left for the academy."

"I was recruited on campus by M.I.G. in my sophomore year. One of the stipulations was that I could have very little contact with home and my family," Ellen said.

"Why would you agree to that?" Toby said.

Ellen grinned. "Do you boys still like James Bond?"

"Do we ever," Shaun said.

"Remember who showed you your first Bond film?"

The memory filled Shaun's mind and he couldn't believe he had ever forgotten about his secret agent, 007 loving babysitter. "It was you. *Moonraker*, I think."

"One of my favorites," Ellen said. "I've dreamed of being an intelligence agent or spy ever since I can remember. When M.I.G. offered to take me in I jumped at the chance. I've seen and done things in the past few years that would make 007 envious."

"Don't you miss home," Toby said.

"Sometimes, but I love what I do and the work M.I.G does is extremely important. They've saved the planet more times than you can imagine. If it wasn't for them, we'd all be staggering in an undead wasteland. But…" her voice trailed off as she thought. Then she continued. "I do miss my family. Have you guys seen my sister?"

"Alice?" Toby said.

Ellen's eyes lit up.

Shaun realized that it was Ellen's eyes, the same eyes that her younger sister Alice had, that had caused his infatuation with both sisters. But Alice's eyes weren't infatuating anymore, and the last time he'd seen her she was undead, gnawing on something nasty.

"Well, we saw her—" Toby started, but Shaun cut him off with an elbow to the side.

"Dude?" Toby grunted.

"She'll be fine when Dr. Romero gives her and everyone else the antidote," Shaun said.

"Yes, of course." Ellen tried to smile, then seemed to change her mind and reached for her coffee.

"Lieutenant Corporal," a voice behind them said. Shaun looked back. The soldier who had escorted them into camp had poked his head inside the tent. "You're needed in the briefing room."

Ellen put the coffee down. "I'm on my way."

The soldier disappeared as quickly as he'd come.

Ellen looked at Dr. Romero. "Doctor, get back to work on the super-antidote. When we get the word that it's okay to break protocol, I want to be ready to move."

Dr. Romero gave a tight-lipped nod and pushed his glasses up. Ellen stepped around the table, and as she made for the exit, she gave Shaun a reassuring squeeze on the shoulder. Shaun smiled at her, but nothing in her face reassured him.

When she was gone, Toby asked Dr. Romero, "What's the super-antidote?"

"A much more potent and faster acting antidote than what I used on myself and the Sheriff. That one had only a fifty percent chance of being effective and only works within a few hours of infection."

"But the super one is a hundred percent?" Sam asked.

Dr. Romero bobbed his head. "Close enough. That reminds me. In order to synthesize our super-antidote, I need something from you, Shaun."

Shaun looked at the doctor. "Me? What?"

Dr. Romero tilted forward and peered over his glasses. "Blood."

In the M.I.G. lab, Shaun sat in a chair as Dr. Romero held up one of the largest needles he'd ever seen. Shaun's last vaccination shot was a few months ago, and the pediatrician said it wouldn't hurt, but of course it did.

"Ah," Shaun said as the doctor tightened the rubber tube around his arm. "Is this gonna hurt?"

"Yes," Dr. Romero said, positioning the needle.

"Wait!" Shaun shrieked. "Aren't you supposed to say no, or you're just going to feel a little stick?"

Dr. Romero sighed. "I'm not a people doctor, I'm a researcher. I mostly work with cadavers or animals. I'm not that practiced with live people, and I'm going to plunge a seven-gauge needle through your skin into a vein and withdraw several vials of your blood. It's going to be uncomfortable, unpleasant, and since it is unlikely I'm going to hit the vein correctly the first time, the experience will definitely be painful. If I said anything less, I'd be lying." Dr. Romero brandished the syringe. "May I proceed?"

"Since you put it that way," Shaun said. "Go right ahead."

Dr. Romero wasn't lying. It hurt, and not just once, as it took him three times to hit a vein. When the blood began to flow, Sam put a hand on Shaun's shoulder and looked at the doctor. "So how exactly is Shaun-juice supposed to help you with the super-cure thing?"

With the first vial filled, Dr. Romero pulled it out and slid in the next. Another flash of pain zipped up Shaun's arm and he closed his eyes. "You're really horrible at this."

"Sorry, Shaun," Dr. Romero said, sincerely. "And to answer your question, Samantha, I have been analyzing Shaun's blood for a few years now."

"You have?" Shaun said, eyes popping open. "How?"

"Ever wonder why every time you go in for your annual physical, your family physician takes a sample of your blood?" Romero said, raising an eyebrow.

"I thought that's just what they did during a physical."

"For adults, yes, but not for kids." Dr. Romero removed the second full vial and snapped in the next. "After your bee attack I asked your father if I could take a look at your blood. I was very interested as to why you survived. By all accounts you shouldn't have."

"Did you know he missed the world record, held by a guy in Africa, by just one sting?" Toby said.

"Yes, in fact I was able to run a comparison with the record-holder's blood. Turns out that prior to your attacks you both possessed a unique ability that is so rare, you and the gentleman in Africa are the only two known humans to have it."

"Which is," Shaun said, beginning to feel like a lab rat.

"A natural resistance to bacteria, viruses, and toxins, specifically bee venom. That's how you survived. But it was after your attack that your blood did something miraculous. You developed antibodies we've never seen before, creating a super-antitoxin that flows through you that's resistant to even the deadliest strains. It even has a regenerative quality, a kind of fast-acting natural healing at the cellular level. And it is this element that will save the people of Honeywell Springs."

"Wicked sick, dude," Toby said. "You have a super power."

"I'd rather have x-ray vision or super-strength, to be honest," Shaun scoffed. "How come I don't know anything about this?"

"Your dad wanted to keep it secret. He hoped to use your blood to help me create new vaccines, and start a new line in your family's company. Ripley's Pharmaceuticals."

Shaun was told the reason his family didn't leave Honeywell Springs was because of their attachment to the town's past, and the truth was his dad just wanted to make future profits from his blood. Shaun felt betrayed.

"I've said it before and I'll say it again," Toby snarled. "Your dad is a jerk."

Sam nodded. "I have to agree with pansy-pants."

Sheriff Rosco put a hand on Shaun's shoulder. "Don't judge him too harshly, Shaun. Most everything your dad does benefits the town."

Shaun clenched his fists tighter. He wanted to scream. Another bolt of pain rocketed up his arm. Dr. Romero was changing vials again. "Hey, Doc, you are going to leave me some, right?"

"Almost done, my boy." Romero chuckled, but instantly swallowed it as Ellen stepped into the lab. Her face was ashen, shoulders slumped. She walked quietly to the group huddled around Shaun.

Ellen leaned against a table and crossed her arms. "They considered Dr. Romero's suggestions, but M.I.G. doesn't have protocols for reversing an outbreak. They did agree to develop some for the future, but that…"

Dr. Romero covered his face with a hand.

"It'll be too late for Honeywell Springs," Shaun said, taking a deep breath.

"So what happens now?" Sam asked.

"In about an hour, we'll begin to fall back to a safe distance," Ellen said.

"Safe from what?" Toby said timidly, as if he didn't really want to know the answer.

"The blast zone," Dr. Romero answered, lowering his hand. "Honeywell Springs is going to be erased."

CHAPTER

17

WIN, LOSE OR DIE

"So what happens to us?" Sheriff Rosco asked.

"Sheriff," Dr. Romero said, motioning with his head toward Sam, Toby and Shaun. "Perhaps we should discuss that later."

"Oh," Sheriff Rosco said, eyeing Shaun. "Of course."

An awful feeling grew in Shaun's stomach. "Wait a minute. What're you guys talking about?"

Dr. Romero and the sheriff exchanged uncomfortable glances.

Shaun looked at Ellen. "What happens to survivors of a town that has been cleansed?"

Ellen looked down at her shoes. "M.I.G. will erase the memories of your lives in Honeywell Springs. You'll be given new identities, deposited into foster families in different parts of the country. You'll most likely never see one another again."

"No way," Toby said. "Erasing memories, that's like science fiction."

Shaun stared at Ellen. Everything about her expression said she was telling the truth. He turned to face Toby. "Dude, we just spent the night running from zombies. I don't think I know what the difference between fiction and non-fiction *is* anymore."

Dr. Romero pulled the needle from Shaun's arm. "You should

consider yourself lucky to have just your memory erased," he said. "The only reason they didn't shoot you three on sight when you drove up was because they were still gathering information. My proposal to reverse the infection was still under consideration. But now that they have reached a decision…"

"They're going to erase our memories," Sheriff Rosco murmured. "Just like the town."

Ellen nodded. "It's M.I.G. protocol."

Sam stepped over to Ellen and punched her on the shoulder. "The people you work with suck!"

Ellen barely reacted. Sam's punch looked to be a good one, but Shaun's former babysitter turned M.I.G. agent just stood there, unmoving. A scarcely noticeable grin curled up one side of her face. Then she leaned forward, encouraging everyone to do the same. She whispered, "As of this second, I don't work with them anymore."

Shaun felt a twinge of hope.

"The bomber won't scramble until just before dawn." Ellen glanced at her watch. "That gives us almost three hours to save Honeywell Springs."

They spent the next ten minutes discussing the plan Dr. Romero had proposed to M.I.G. He'd offered them the option of neutralizing all the zombies in Honeywell Springs with a specially developed chemical smoker. It worked like a regular bee smoker, which puts bumblebees to sleep so honey can be harvested from a hive. Instead of harvesting honey, Dr. Romero and M.I.G. would administer the super-antidote to all the neutralized zombies. But M.I.G. had problems with the plan, and decided to stick with the cleansing protocol.

"So the main obstacle your M.I.G friends had with the doctor's idea is a delivery system for the Doc's smoker solution," Sheriff Rosco said, rubbing one of his chins.

Ellen said, "We discussed delivering the smoke in agricultural helicopters, like spraying pesticides on a field, but there's no way to guarantee getting all the zombies at once. If there was a way to congregate them in one area, it could still work."

"You mean like the theater?" Shaun said.

"I guess that could work, but how to get them inside?" Ellen said.

Shaun grinned knowingly at Toby and Sam. "I think most of them are already in there, along with some of the Doc's giant bees."

"What are you saying?" Dr. Romero said.

Shaun told the adults what they'd noticed when they were trapped on the store roof, how the zombies seemed to hide and coordinate their attacks, walk in lines, and move in and out of the theater like it was some kind of zombie home base.

Dr. Romero sat down and steepled his fingers under his chin. "M.I.G has never dealt with this kind of zombie before. The insect DNA is transforming its human host. They're not just zombies, but zombie bee hybrids. Zom*Bees*."

"So they're part bumblebee," Ellen said.

Dr. Romero said, "Yellowjacket, phorid fly, even hornet. I used DNA from all of them in the development of *Apis mellifera gigantus*."

"The what?" Sam said.

"Giant monster bees," Shaun said.

"It's the reason I know the smokers will work and it's why the infected are exhibiting more and more insect-like behavior." He dropped his hands with a smile. "They're evolving a hive mentality. They may be unaware of what they're doing, letting their new instincts drive them into creating a zombee hive. The Honeywell Community Theater, a place they may remember gathering with friends and loved ones, has become that hive."

"That would explain why satellite imaging shows most of them staying within a few blocks of the theater," Ellen said.

"Some of the drones have become foragers, scouts," Dr. Romero said, "working for the benefit of the hive."

"Let's say we get them all in the theater," Shaun said. "How will the helicopters be able to spray them to put them to sleep?"

"They can't," Ellen said.

Sheriff Rosco snapped his fingers. "They don't have to. Doc, the town's emergency plan, remember?"

Dr. Romero slapped his forehead. "How could I forget? The emergency plan, of course."

"Emergency plan?" Sam said.

Sheriff Rosco leaned forward. "About twenty years ago there was a lot of paranoia about the number of bees in town. At any one time there are more bees in and around Honeywell Springs than there are people on the entire planet. If all those bees suddenly turned on us, we'd be up the creek without a banjo."

"Could that really happen?" Toby said.

"Trust a guy who has been attacked by a swarm," Shaun interjected. "It could happen. I've been having nightmares about it for the last five years."

"In the town's emergency plan, in case of a massive bee swarm, the theater is equipped with industrial-sized smokers. The biggest ever built," Sheriff Rosco said. "The entire building could be used as a trap to attract and neutralize a swarm."

"I formulated a special paint for the theater's interior with bee pheromone that can attract a swarm. The average bee going about its business in Honeywell Springs wouldn't pay the theater much attention, but an agitated swarm would find it irresistible," Dr. Romero said. "The bee pheromone may also be the reason our infected friends chose the theater as their hive."

"What about the stragglers?" Ellen said. "Those foragers and scouts. How can we bring them all to the theater?"

"Well, they will chase the uninfected," Dr. Romero said.

"So we have to use ourselves as bait?" Sheriff Rosco's voice rose.

Dr. Romero bobbed his head looking as if he were trying to come up with an alternative.

"Hey, Doc," Shaun said. "The past few weeks I've noticed you've ordered a lot of meat. Does it have anything to do with the giant bees?"

"Yes. *Apis mellifera gigantus* has a voracious appetite. It's probably how the infected inherited flesh-eating, zombie-like behavior."

Shaun grinned. "Well, I think I have an idea on how to gather up our stragglers." Shaun told everyone his idea. They agreed it was a gamble, but worth a try. With most of their plan in place, only one detail was left to figure out. Who was going?

The three adults talked among themselves and even though Shaun, Sam, and Toby were sitting right there, Shaun felt they were being excluded from this final detail. Somehow the adults had already decided that the kids were staying behind, while one or two of the adults snuck out of camp to save Honeywell Springs.

Shaun listened quietly for a few minutes, knowing that what the grownups were planning wouldn't work. Ellen and Dr. Romero had to stay here, and the Sheriff, a man who weighed over three-hundred pounds, would be unable to keep ahead of the zombees. Shaun realized he would have to go back to Honeywell Springs.

"Hey," Shaun interrupted. "Let's get real. It's obvious who needs to go. Dr. Romero has to stay here and work on the super-antidote." Shaun met Ellen's gaze. "You *have* to stay, because if we're successful, you're the only one who has a chance of convincing M.I.G. to stop the bombs." Shaun swiveled to look at the sheriff. "And no offence, sir, these things don't move fast, but they keep coming and don't get tired."

"I'm in better shape than I look," Sheriff Rosco said sheepishly.

"Ah, Shaun," Toby said. "Can I speak to you over here a second? You too, Sam."

The three stepped over to the other side of the lab, just out of earshot.

"Hey, I'm all for saving our hometown and all," Toby said. "But shouldn't a grownup do it? We're just kids."

"C'mon, dude," Shaun said. "Remember back at the Doc's house when we decided to head back into town and warn everyone? We were going to be heroes, man. This is no different."

"I thought we decided to get out of his house so that creepy Bumblebeeder thing didn't come after us."

Shaun shrugged. "That too. But listen, us three going is the best bet that Honeywell Springs has. What other choice is there?"

"We fold, man. Get the heck out of here," Toby said. "We tell them we're going to town then split. Run as far away as possible. Then run some more."

"Dude, we're thirteen years old. Where're we gonna go?"

"You'll be fourteen in like a month," Toby said.

"Look, if you guys want to run, fine," Sam said. "But I'm going back."

Shaun wasn't sure but Sam's eyes looked teary.

"After my mom died," she continued, "things were pretty rough for me and my dad. But that little bee-crazy town took us in. Dad got a nice job, and things got better. Not perfect, but better. My dad is the only family I got, and if there's a chance I can save him, even a slim one, I'm taking it. For me it's all or nothing."

Shaun didn't know any of this about Sam. At the moment he wasn't too fond of his parents but he couldn't imagine losing either of them. Shaun wanted to put his hand on her shoulder or offer her a hug. But he was pretty sure she'd punch him if he did.

Sam wiped her nose and sniffled. Then she looked at Shaun, her gaze steely.

Shaun smiled. "I'm with you, Sam."

They both turned to Toby.

Toby rolled his eyes. "Fine," he said. "I was only kidding about the running away plan." Toby pointed a finger at both of them. "But if you guys get me killed, I'm never speaking to either of you again."

"Is that a promise?" Sam said, grinning.

"Ha, ha," Toby said.

"So we're doing this," Shaun said.

Sam and Toby nodded.

"Now, let's go convince the grownups," Shaun said.

It took far less convincing than Shaun thought. Apparently Ellen had come to the same conclusion, but she insisted that Sheriff Rosco go as well. He was one of the figureheads in town who knew how to operate the emergency smoker system in the theater, so it made sense. Everyone agreed.

Ellen then excused herself, saying she needed to check on a few things. While she was gone Sheriff Rosco explained to Toby, Shaun and Sam how to operate the smoker system in case he didn't make it to the theater. Dr. Romero then demonstrated how to fill the smoker tanks with the new agent he'd developed to neutralize the zombees. It would be carried in two canisters which he slipped into a backpack and handed to Shaun. As Shaun looped his arms through the straps, Ellen returned. Her expression looked urgent.

"They're gonna start tearing down the camp in five minutes. It's gonna get real chaotic around here during the bug-out," she said. "It's the perfect time to make our move. Here, put these on." She handed out what looked like futuristic wristwatches.

"What're they for?" Shaun said.

"They'll mask your heat signature from our satellites. To the M.I.G. personnel monitoring the town you'll appear just like any other room-temperature zombee."

Toby admired the watch. "Total 007, man."

Shaun strapped it around his wrist, as did the other three. He noticed the display, red digital numbers: *2 hr 18 min 43 sec.* "What're these numbers ticking backwards?"

"It's a countdown. I set them to reach zero at dawn. When it reaches zero—"

"Kabluey," Sam interrupted.

Fantastic, Shaun thought. *We have just over two hours to do the impossible.*

"How do you know they'll wait until dawn?" Sam asked.

"Standard protocol," Ellen answered. "First light allows for maximum visual assessment of damage. Obliteration must be total and complete."

"Very nice," Sam said. "Sorry I asked."

"How can we let you know if we're successful?" Toby said.

Ellen pointed to the gold button on Shaun's device. "Press that and you can use the device like a walkie-talkie. I'll be monitoring the frequency. Don't press it unless you have to."

"Why not?" Sheriff Rosco said.

"Activation of the communicator turns the watch into a beacon. M.I.G. will be able to pinpoint your location."

"And we don't want that until we're done," Shaun said.

Toby pulled the collar of his grey jumpsuit away from his neck. "Hey, Ellen, do you have anything else for us to wear? These suits are kind of warm."

Shaun agreed. It felt like he was in a winter track suit.

Ellen shook her head. "Trust me," she said. "You want to stay in these. They're similar to the kind of shark suits divers wear, but vastly improved by M.I.G. They're made from the most bite-resistant technology ever conceived."

"Wow," Toby said, touching the material on his sleeve and meeting Shaun's gaze. "Anti-zombie suits, super-spy watches, and a mission to save our hometown. We're so MI-6 right now."

Shaun smiled, feeling Toby's enthusiasm.

"Okay, dweebs," Sam said. "Let's do this."

Shaun looked at the display on the watch: 2 hours, 17 minutes and counting. He hoped that a cool watch, zombie suits and enthusiasm would be enough, because if it wasn't Shaun and everyone he had ever known had two hours to exist.

CHAPTER

18

LICENCE TO KILL

Ellen was right. The camp was in disarray. Soldiers moved about like army ants, hustling, tearing things down, and packing up the camp. It was the perfect time to slip out. The sheriff led the way through the camp, with Shaun, Toby and Sam in his enormous shadow. Since they didn't have time to hoof it back into town, the plan was to sneak into the camp's motor pool—an area where all the vehicles were kept—and steal a Humvee.

The kids stayed low, moving from spot to spot, but the sheriff was too big to conceal himself. Shaun got the feeling that Sheriff Rosco was going to get them all caught before they'd even begun. As they moved Shaun motioned to Toby and Sam to hang back. His friends clearly understood and the three ducked behind a collection of oil drums.

The sheriff blundered forward, no longer bothering to stay out of sight. He reached the entrance of the motor pool, marked by a few orange cones, and stopped to glance back. Toby was about to stand up and join him but Shaun grabbed his arm. Two soldiers exiting the motor pool had surprised the sheriff from behind, one brandishing his rifle.

"Halt," the solider said. "Where do you think you're going?"

"I… I was looking for the lab," Sheriff Rosco said. "I'm supposed to meet—"

"The lab is back that way," the soldier barked, aiming the muzzle of the rifle at the sheriff's wide chest. The two soldiers exchanged glances, and Shaun got the sudden feeling that they were going to shoot him, right there on the spot.

"Good job, gentlemen." Ellen stepped from the shadows. "I thought this one might try to bolt."

The soldiers eyed her suspiciously as she approached.

"He and Dr. Romero were cooking up some sort of plan." Ellen pulled out a pair of handcuffs.

"Ah, Lieutenant Corporal," the soldier pointing the rifle said. "Should we evacuate him now? I mean—"

"Negative," Ellen commanded. "Major Captain has a few more questions for him." As she snapped on the cuffs, she slipped off the Sheriff's M.I.G. wristwatch, then tossed it into the dark. "You won't need to know what time it is anymore," she snarled. "Why don't you two head toward the lab and look for the doctor?"

"I got a better idea." The soldier said this disrespectfully as he slung his rifle over a shoulder. "Why don't we go with you and the prisoner and talk to Major Captain. We'll let him sort this all out."

Ellen shrugged. "Fine by me. It's your careers." She turned abruptly and yanked on the sheriff's cuffs, moving away. The soldiers followed close behind. It was obvious they didn't believe her, and Shaun's stomach burned at the thought of what they'd do when they found out she was lying.

When Ellen passed the spot where the three had crouched, she made brief eye contact with Shaun. The message in her gaze was clear. *Here's your chance—get moving!*

"Come on," Shaun whispered.

"Wait," Toby said. "I was okay with going to save the town and the world and all as long as we had adult supervision. But it's just *us* now."

"He would have only slowed us down, man," Shaun said.

"Yeah," Sam said. "Come on, pansy-pants. Do you want to live forever?"

"Yes," Toby said. "I really, really do."

Shaun put up his fist for a bump. "Come on. It's James Bond time."

Smiling, Toby gave in. "Fine. Live and let die, bro." He bumped his friend's fist, then looked at Sam. "Does that make you a Bond girl?"

Sam narrowed her eyes. "In your dreams, dweeb." She got up. "Come on, before they come back."

It was a good bet that the two soldiers the sheriff bumped into were the motor pool guards, because they saw no one else when they snuck in. Shaun stopped at the closest Humvee, and his foot bumped something. It was the sheriff's M.I.G. wristwatch Ellen had tossed. It was a suspicious thing to do, but Shaun figured she was trying to get rid of evidence that involved her. He snatched it up and stuck it in his pocket, then waited for the others to catch up. Sam passed him and waved him forward. Shaun realized that the Humvee was going to make noise, and the more distance they had from the camp and its guns, the better.

After zigzagging between the trucks, transports and other military vehicles, Sam stopped at a Hummer, at least a hundred yards from where they'd come in. She opened the door and they all got in. As Ellen had said, the keys were on the dashboard. It was M.I.G. protocol. In the event of the camp being overrun by zombies, the first one to an escape vehicle became the driver. No one had to wait around for keys.

As Sam slid behind the wheel, Shaun glimpsed uncertainty in her eyes.

"You can drive this, right?" he whispered.

"I can drive anything," she snapped, looking around, exploring the controls with her fingertips. "Just give me a minute."

Shaun looked at the countdown on his wristwatch. 1 hour, 58 minutes, and ticking. "We don't exactly have a lot of those."

"Okay," Sam said. "Seatbelts buckled, and hold on." She fired up the Hummer, and Shaun felt hopeful as the first part of their plan seemed to be working. The good feeling disappeared when sparks danced over the Humvee's hood with a metallic *pang*.

"What was that?" Toby said.

As if in answer, gunfire echoed behind them, and more sparks flashed on the hood.

"They're *shooting* at us?" Toby yelled. Shaun and Toby turned around. The two soldiers who had confronted the sheriff were running at them, firing their rifles. Bullets ricocheted off the Hummer's reinforced armor plating. *Ping, pang, pop.*

"Wow, they seem mad!" Toby said.

"Go, Sam, go," Shaun screamed.

The Humvee lurched forward, and Sam spun the wheel.

Shaun realized Sam wasn't heading back toward the entrance. "Where're you going?"

Sam pointed ahead into the forest.

"There's no road!" Shaun said.

"We can't go back through the camp now," Sam said. "They're trying to kill us."

Heavy thumps pounded the roof as a spray of automatic weapon fire found its target.

Toby covered his head. "She has a point, dude! Those are not warning shots!"

Shaun braced his hands on the dashboard. "I hope you know what you're doing."

"You and me both, dweeb."

The Hummer sped out of the motor pool clearing and into the forest. Thick bushes collapsed under the front bumper, and the vehicle bounced like it was on a trampoline. Shaun felt like he was going to be ejected at any moment.

Sam slowed down and flicked on the headlights. The beams were bright and enabled her to steer around the trees. Her knuckles went white trying to keep the vehicle under control.

Shaun was impressed at her strength. He was even more impressed that she seemed to know where she was going, as her turns missed trees.

"You know where you're going?" Shaun asked.

"Dad and I ride motorcycles back here," Sam said. "There's a trail up this way. It leads all the way to town."

Toby slapped the dashboard. "That's awesome."

"It won't make any difference," she said, "if we don't lose those guys."

"What guys?" Shaun said.

"Behind us," Sam said.

The boys turned and looked out the back window. A set of headlights bounced a hundred yards behind them in hot pursuit.

CHAPTER

19

A HARD MAN TO KILL

Shaun couldn't believe the M.I.G. soldiers were actually coming after them.

"How're they even following us in this mess?" Toby said.

"It's our headlights," Shaun said. "Hey, Sam, when you get to this trail, do you know it well enough to follow it with the headlights off?"

Sam shrugged. "We can find out."

"Good enough," Shaun said. "Let me know when we're close."

"You got a plan for losing them?" Toby said.

Shaun nodded, feeling his chest tighten. He reached into his pocket, pulled out his new inhaler and was about to take a hit.

"Just about there," Sam said.

Shaun put the inhaler back unused and pulled out the sheriff's wristwatch. "Okay, kill the lights and stop. Toby, open the window."

Sam and Toby followed instructions, and in seconds the Humvee skidded to a stop on the forest floor.

"Here goes nothing." Shaun turned the wristwatch and pressed the gold button on its side. The display lit up, revealing a tiny microphone.

Shaun took a deep breath, then spoke rapidly, panicked. "Ellen,

Ellen, we need help. The Humvee slid down a hillside. Toby is hurt real bad, man. He's not moving. I think he might be… Oh, God, he might be dead. We need help! I'm scared, Ellen. Please come get us…" Shaun chucked the device out the window. It tumbled down a thickly forested slope.

"Genius, man," Sam said. "You think they'll follow the beacon?"

"You want to sit here and find out?" Shaun asked.

"Heck no!" Sam took her foot off the brake, and sped toward the trail. When they turned onto the dirt road, the Humvee finally stopped bouncing. No one was in danger of flying out of their seat anymore. Shaun was more concerned about Sam running into a tree with the headlights out. But her knowledge of where they were and the thin slivers of starlight were enough to keep them from crashing.

No one spoke. Shaun felt tense, scared, and he wondered if any of them would see another sunrise. He reached for his inhaler again but realized he didn't need it. He was fine. He took a deep breath, hoping to relieve some tension.

"I think it worked," Sam said, her voice shaky. "They're not following."

"Hey," Toby said harshly. "Why was I the one that had to die?"

"What?" Shaun said.

"In your little message to the M.I.G. guys," Toby said, then mimicked Shaun. "Oh, Ellen, Toby might be dead."

"You're not really dead, ya dork."

"I didn't like hearing you say I was." Toby folded his arms and frowned. He looked as scared and tired as Shaun felt. "Next time we're in this situation, kill someone else."

"Promise, dude." Shaun chuckled. "Next time we're under fire in a stolen jeep heading toward a town overrun by zombees, I'll use someone else's…" Shaun couldn't finish because he was laughing too hard.

Toby's frown melted away, and he laughed too.

"Oh, God," Sam said, shaking her head. "I really do hate you both."

Thirty minutes later Shaun and Toby were in the cargo compartment of the delivery truck they'd seen earlier, steadying themselves as Sam drove the big box truck. The boys tossed out honeydogs and watched as zombees scrambled to scoop them up.

"Hey, it's working," Toby said. "It's really working." Toby threw an entire case out. Before the soggy box stopped rolling, three zombee drones tore it open. The wet cardboard fell away like an animal shedding unwanted skin, and they sunk their infected teeth into the honey-dipped meat.

"Got to hand it to you, Shaun, this was a great idea."

"I have my moments." Shaun braced himself on a stack of boxes as Sam shifted gears. Zombees were gathering around the box Toby had tossed out and he realized this could be a problem. Shaun's idea of using the honeydog delivery truck to lure the infected people of Honeywell Springs to the theater wouldn't work if they over-baited the trail. "Dude, don't throw out any more whole cases. Just toss a few dogs out at a time, like breadcrumbs, so they'll stay with the truck."

"Good call," Toby said, handing Shaun a fistful of dogs. Shaun couldn't stand these things. The honey-enriched hot dogs and honey-glazed corn dogs, had always made him queasy.

"How many do you think are following us so far?" Toby said.

Shaun knelt and did a fast zombee headcount. "Two, maybe three hundred. It's too dark to tell."

Toby crouched next to Shaun looking out at the black-and-yellow swarm staggering after the truck. The creatures only stopped following to scoop up a honeydog or fight one another for the meaty breadcrumbs. But not all of them tore into the meat. Some zombees just gathered them, stuffed them in pockets. *Foragers and scouts,* Shaun thought. *They're as much bees as they are zombies.*

As Sam made a right turn, Shaun steadied himself again. She shifted gears, and he marveled at her ability to drive almost anything. She'd done a great job so far, slowly circling the blocks around Main Street and gathering all the zombee scouts and foragers.

"I count about four hundred," Toby said, chucking out a few more honeydogs.

Shaun glanced at the countdown on his wristwatch. *Fifty-two minutes until dawn. Fifty-two minutes until M.I.G. vaporizes Honeywell Springs.* "We'd better head toward the theater."

"Aww," Toby moaned. "This is kinda fun. Like feeding ducks. Great big, creepy, monstrous, zombiefied ducks."

The truck's engine stuttered, and it felt like they were slowing down.

"Sam, what was that?" Shaun yelled. The truck had a small sliding window that allowed them to see Sam behind the wheel from their spot in the cargo bed.

"We're running out of gas," Sam said over her shoulder.

"Man." Shaun slapped his hand on the cold floor. "Do we have enough to make it to the theater?"

"Uh…" Sam turned and glanced nervously at Shaun. By the look in her eye, the answer was either no or she had no idea. Either way, things were going south.

The truck jolted, causing Shaun and Toby to grab the wall. A pair of hands slapped the truck's back bumper, and Shaun and Toby exchanged panicked glances.

"There're catching up," Toby said.

Shaun swallowed hard. "Which means we're going too slow." He stepped forward and kicked at the zombee holding onto the bumper, but it held tight. Shaun took aim and kicked the center of its black-and-yellow-striped shirt. The zombee fell back, bounced off those behind it, then dropped to its knees. Toby chucked out a half-full box of honeydogs. It landed where the zombee fell. In seconds, a dozen clambered around, tearing apart the opened box. Soggy honeydogs spilled out onto the street and rolled in all directions.

"Nice, job," Shaun said.

"Why isn't Sam heading straight back to the theater?" Toby said. "If we're running out of gas, shouldn't she take the shortest route?"

Toby was right. The fastest way to the theater was down Pollen Street, but Sam had just passed it. Shaun ran to the front of the truck and stuck his face in the opening. "Sam, where're you going?"

Sam pounded the steering wheel with a fist. "Come on," she said as the truck went into a new round of sputters.

"Sam!" Shaun yelled.

"If we can make it to the top of Honeycomb Avenue," Sam yelled back. "We can coast all the way down to Main and the theater."

"Did she say coast?" Toby asked.

Shaun nodded, trying to understand Sam's reasoning. Then it hit him. Honeycomb Avenue was on a hill that descended to Main Street. Sam wanted to use the truck's momentum to carry them the rest of the way. It was a longer route, but with their gas situation it was one that had a better chance of succeeding.

"Did that make sense to you?" Toby said.

"Yes. Sam is pretty smart."

Toby displayed an I-told-ya-so grin. "She's starting to grow on you, isn't she?"

Shaun snorted. "Yeah, like fungus, or a flesh-eating virus."

"Hey, dweebs," Sam shouted. "I can *hear* you!"

The engine roared then sputtered.

The truck slowed, and Shaun looked out the back. Hundreds of zombees staggered just a dead arm's-length behind the truck. If they stopped moving, the infected townsfolk of Honeywell Springs would swarm into the back of the truck, and it would be all over.

"How much farther," Shaun yelled.

"Just… a few more… feet," Sam grunted as if willing the truck forward. She turned the wheel hard to the right. "Yes! We made it."

Shaun high-fived Toby as the truck started to pick up speed. The zombees seemed to all realize the truck was moving away. The horde started to jog after the truck, some leaping forward and grabbing the bumper. The boys tossed out more honeydogs, keeping the swarming mob of zombees on their tail, but at a safe distance. There were hundreds with their bouncing antennas, some illuminated with tiny LEDs, like a macabre festival of shambling lights parade.

Shaun scanned the buildings outside. They were on Main Street, coasting through the festival area. Zombees emerged from alleyways and from behind concession carts and started after the truck. In a few seconds the hundreds that followed them swelled to almost a thousand, and the sight made Shaun's heart pound so hard he thought it might burst from his chest.

"Uh, guys," Sam yelled over her shoulder. "Hold on!"

"Why?" Shaun said.

Before Sam answered, the truck jolted up. Shaun peered through the opening to the driver's compartment and through the windshield. He glimpsed pieces of a cotton candy stand falling from the hood. They approached another mobile kiosk, honey-dipped corn on the cob.

"Can't you go around?" Shaun said, trying to quell the panic in his voice.

Sam said, "Not without slowing us down too much."

Shaun looked away as they plowed into the food cart, dozens of corn cobs pelting the windshield, honey streaking the glass. They clipped another cart, and its fragments scraped along the outside like claws.

"Well, crashing into them can't be helping us go faster," Shaun said as Sam managed to avoid a honeydog stand. "Hey, you *missed* one."

"Stop backseat driving," Sam yelled. "We're here!"

The truck skidded as Sam hit the brake and spun the wheel. The back of the truck whipped around. Shaun's whole world went into a tailspin. The boys fell to the floor and rolled like bowling balls down an alley.

"What is going on?" Toby yelled.

Trying to sit up, Shaun thrust his thumb over his shoulder. "I don't know. Ask stunt-girl up there."

The truck slammed to a stop. Shaun and Toby stared out the back at a set of double doors only ten feet away. It was the entryway to the Honeywell Community Theater.

"Damn, she did it," Shaun said. But before anyone could celebrate, zombees poured from the theater doors like attacking hornets from a nest. The zombees that had followed the truck began climbing in, crawling over each other to get inside.

Shaun and Toby ran to the front and tossed boxes of honeydogs back to create an obstacle. The freshly thawed meat caught the swarm's attention and the zombees tore into the boxes. The boys hustled through the opening and joined Sam in the driver's compartment. Shaun reached back and shut the door between them and the zombees, then turned the deadbolt. The sound of hands slapping the outside of the truck filled the cab.

"Okay," Sam said. "I got us here. Now what?"

Zombees surrounded the truck. Everywhere Shaun looked,

hungry eyes met his gaze.

"Uh," Shaun started, but a beeping seized his attention. He looked down. Green letters flashed on his M.I.G. wristwatch: *INCOMING TRANSMISSION.*

Shaun raised his wrist and pressed the gold button. "Hello."

The watch transmitted a voice. "Shaun, this is Ellen. What's your status?"

Status? Shaun thought. *Is surrounded by flesh eating zombees a status?*

"Ah, you know," he stammered, "could be better." The mass of zombees started rocking the truck. "A lot better, actually," he added.

"Is anyone hurt?"

"No, but—"

"That was a pretty smart move using the sheriff's watch as a decoy," Ellen said. "You impressed Major Captain."

"Is that a good thing?"

"Yes. And just to let you know, I got them to give you guys a chance. Our satellite images show every infected resident of Honeywell Springs has converged on your location."

Several bloody hands slapped the window next to Shaun. He jumped. "No kidding."

"But you need to hurry," Ellen said, her voice sounding dire. "The bomber is already in the air."

Jeez, Shaun thought. *No pressure!*

CHAPTER

20

THE WORLD IS NOT ENOUGH

Toby, Sam and Shaun sat motionless in the truck's cab. The sound of the zombees pounding on the outside was a thunderous roar. Ellen was still talking, but none of them were listening.

"Shaun," Ellen said. "Are you still there? Shaun. Sh—"

Shaun tapped the gold button, cutting her off. "Boring conversation anyway."

"Well, guys," Sam said. "What do you want to do?"

Toby turned to Sam. "Hey, you didn't call us dweebs."

"What can I say? You guys are growing on me. Like fungus."

Shaun smiled and felt surprisingly calm, given the circumstances. "The way I see it, we have two choices."

"Yeah?" Sam said.

"A: We stay here, safe, warm, and perfectly healthy, for the rest of our lives. Which will last about," Shaun glanced at the countdown on his wristwatch. "Twenty-two minutes."

Sam and Toby chuckled uncomfortably.

"Or, B: We go out there fighting and try to save the world, or at least enough to save our little town. We'll most likely be torn to pieces before we get ten feet. Kind of a horrible way to die."

"Maybe not," Toby said.

"Yes it is," Sam said. "Being torn apart *is* a horrible way to die."

"Well, duh." Toby grabbed a pinch of material on his shoulder. "Super anti-zombie suits, remember?" Toby held his arm in front of Shaun's face. "Go ahead, bite me, dude."

Shaun shook his head. "No way, man."

"Go ahead— oooouuch!"

Sam stopped biting Toby's shoulder and rubbed her lips.

"What was that for?" Toby said.

"Just testing the suit, like you wanted." Sam leaned forward to inspect the spot she'd bit.

"Well?" Shaun inquired.

"Didn't bite through, and my teeth kind of hurt," Sam said. "We'll definitely last longer with these zombie suits."

Shaun said, "Maybe it will be long enough." He leaned against the glass and peered up. Sam had driven the truck to the theater's entryway, with its cargo side wedged under the huge overhanging marquee. Normally it would advertise the name of whatever play the community theater troupe was mangling that month, but now big black letters spelled out, WELCOME TO HONEYWELL SPRINGS – HONEY BEE CAPITAL OF THE WORLD.

Shaun looked at his friends. "Are you guys in the mood for a climb?"

Shaun lowered the truck's window halfway, then he and Toby climbed onto the roof of the cab. The boys had managed this easily as the cab was high enough to be a tough grab for the zombees. But after watching the boys escape their grasp, the infected had gotten smarter. Several stepped up onto the truck's running boards and seized Sam around the waist.

Toby and Shaun strained as they gripped Sam's wrists and pulled. Shaun pulled with all his might, but he could feel Sam slipping. The zombees were adding their weight to the tug of war, and they were winning.

"Just let me go, guys," Sam yelled.

"No way!" Toby said.

"I'm serious," Sam said. "You guys can still make it if you go now. So go!"

"Stop bossing us around," Shaun grunted.

"Yeah," Toby said. "No man left behind."

"Or, annoying, bossy, pain-in-the-butt girls, either," Shaun said. "Will you kick them or something?"

Sam pulled her feet free of the window and kicked out, hard. Her right foot smacked the side of Mayor Savini's head. His black antenna-sprouting top-hat flew off into the darkness, followed immediately by the mayor's round body. Sam kicked again with both feet, sending other zombees tumbling back into the swarm.

Shaun and Toby finally yanked Sam to the roof.

"Thanks, guys," Sam said. "Now what?"

Shaun checked the straps on his backpack, which held Dr. Romero's special smoker solution, and took a deep breath. "Follow me," he said, turning to lead the way. He stepped up onto the roof of the truck's cargo bay, then wedged his shoe into a groove of the theater's marquee. In two minutes the three managed to scale the big sign and climb onto the balcony catwalk that employees used to change the letters on the sign.

They caught their breath and looked down. The swarm of zombees surrounding the truck was now moving inside the theater. Shaun didn't know if they were determined to continue the chase or if it was something else, but either way it was good news. If this was going to work, all the zombees needed to be inside.

Shaun glanced at his wristwatch. *Seventeen minutes and counting.*

They hurried to a small door. It only opened from the inside, but Sam kicked it off its tiny hinges. The small wooden frame splintered apart, making a lot of noise as the door fell inward. They hunkered down to move through a passageway, only a few feet high. A curtain blocked the passage's exit and Shaun crouched next to the material. He swept the cloth to the side and peeked out.

He fell back and sat down.

"How bad?" Toby sounded like he didn't really want to know the answer.

"Imagine the worst possible situation," Shaun said, "and multiple that by three thousand. Give or take."

"Oh, come on." Sam leaned forward to take a look. "How bad could it… Oh, man, it's a packed house."

They were at the rear of the second balcony. Forty rows of seats lay between them and the balcony's edge, a drop-off to the main floor. For every seat in the theater there seemed to be two or three zombees. They could see little of what was below or of the stage from their position, but Shaun had no doubt that every square inch of the theater was crawling. Shaun glanced at the countdown. *Fourteen minutes.*

"Come on guys," Sam said. "To be honest, I didn't think we'd make it this far."

"True." Toby pointed to a small room with dark windows on the other side of the balcony. "That's the control room."

"That's where Sheriff Rosco said the activation switches for the smokers are," Sam said. "What else is in there?"

"It's where they run the lights and sound effects," Toby said. "I was with my dad when he installed a new audio board. You can see out, but the audience can't see in. The windows only let light pass one way."

"We need to get there, and we don't have time to find a safe way," Shaun said. "Everybody ready?" Sam and Toby nodded. Shaun gave them an encouraging smile, and then the three took stance like sprinters at the starting line. "Ready, set, try not to die, and *GO!*"

They bolted around the curtain and ran along the back row. Zombees immediately turned their way and reached out, but their

M.I.G. zombie suits were hard to grasp. They zipped around the horde, each on their own path. An arm wrapped around Shaun's neck, but he bent his knees and spun out of the zombee's embrace. Sam and Toby followed Shaun's lead as he stepped up on the back of the final row of seats. They jumped over three seats, landing in the balcony's center aisle.

Sam and Toby landed behind him with two quick thuds on the plush red carpet, bounding to their feet like practiced tumblers. Shaun sprinted the last ten feet to the control room, ducking beneath grasping arms and claw-like hands. He hit the control room door, which flew inward. He held it wide for Sam and Toby who dove inside. Then Shaun slammed the door shut and pressed himself against it.

Sam and Toby slid a shelf up against the door as Shaun flipped the deadbolt. They all slumped to the floor, to catch their breath. Toby was breathing as hard as he was, but Sam made a different sound.

With a painful expression, she held her wrist to her chest and whimpered. Blood dripped down her suit.

Shaun stared at the bite marks on her hand.

She wiped away a tear. "I'm sorry, guys. I wasn't fast enough."

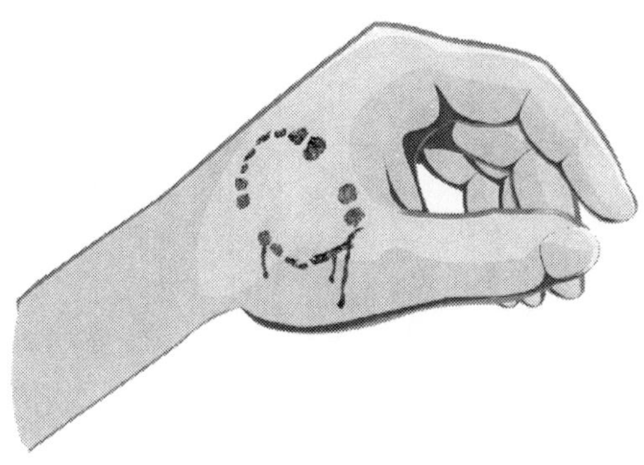

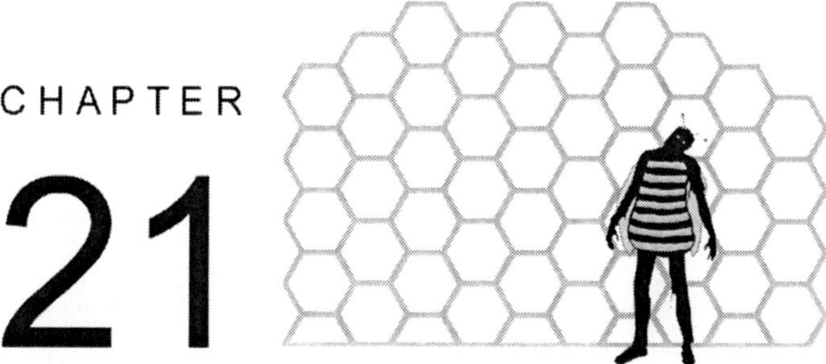

CHAPTER 21

NOBODY LIVES FOREVER

"Does it hurt?" Shaun said.

"Strangely, no," Sam said. "Feels like my whole arm is going numb." Sam slumped against the wall and Toby rushed to her side. "I'm fine," she snapped, but didn't push Toby away when he put his arm around her.

Toby propped her up and Sam's head swiveled to face him.

"You're such a dweeb," she said, her voice shaky.

"I know," he replied.

Shaun turned away. If Sam was dying, and that was a good bet, he had no idea what to say to her. He looked out the control room window, trying to gather his thoughts, and something bizarre caught his attention. "Oh my God, what the heck is that?"

Toby helped Sam over to where Shaun was, and they all looked down at the stage. Most of the curtains and backdrops had been torn away to make room for a massive honeycomb. It looked like the one in Dr. Romero's lab but its hexagon-shaped tunnels were big enough for human beings. The zombees moved toward the stage in orderly lines and worked on a section of the hive, then moved off, as several of Dr. Romero's giant bees buzzed about. It looked as if there were only three of the giant bees left, and although Shaun couldn't be positive, it appeared that they were in charge.

"Just when you think things can't get any weirder," Toby said.

"What's it all for?" Sam said.

Shaun shook his head. "No idea, but remember the doctor said they probably don't even know why they're creating a hive. They're just going on instinct now."

"Freaky," Toby said.

Sam suddenly fell against the lighting board. "I don't feel so good."

Toby rolled a chair toward her and she flopped into it. "Hang in there, Sam." Toby turned to Shaun. "I'll stay here with her and turn the smokers on."

"And where am I going?"

Toby pointed over the zombee hive. "Sheriff Rosco said the main tank is over the stage up by the catwalks. When you get Dr. Romero's solution in, let me know and I'll power up the smokers."

"How can I let you know?"

Toby glanced around, then stepped over to a shelf. He picked up two headsets and handed one to Shaun. "The stage director uses these to talk backstage." Toby reached for another one and said over his shoulder, "Hey, Sam you want one?"

Sam didn't respond. Shaun looked back. She was slumped over the control panel, her hands dangling toward the floor. Toby ran over to her and pushed her back in the chair. "She's not breathing, man." Toby gently tapped her cheek with his hand. "Sam, come on. Sam."

In the back of his mind he'd known that their mission to save Honeywell Springs was most likely a one way trip, but watching Sam slip away was harder than Shaun imagined. He felt sick. He wanted to grieve. He wanted to let Toby grieve, but there wasn't time. He walked over and put a hand on Toby's shoulder. "Dude."

Toby didn't turn around. He just bent forward and wiped his eyes. He then stood up slowly. "Okay, bro. Let's finish this."

Toby booted up the power, and lights flickered on the control room boards. He spoke into his headset and the tiny speakers next to Shaun's ears boomed. "Testing, testing."

"Too loud," Shaun said.

Toby pointed to the volume switch on the headset's power box, hooked to Shaun's belt. Shaun rotated the dial.

"Better?" Toby said.

"Much." Shaun looked at his wristwatch. *Twelve minutes. We're never gonna make it.*

"We got plenty of time," Toby said. "Just get that stuff in the tank, and I'll do the rest."

Shaun pointed at the red metal box on the wall. "Sure you know how to work that thing?"

Toby moved to the box and opened the red door. "Absolutely. Here's the power, and here is the on-off switch."

Shaun looked at the bank of switches, dials, and gauges, and hoped Toby was being truthful. They had no time for mistakes.

"If not," Toby said, pulling out a black three-ring binder, "here's the instruction manual. I'll flip through it while you're climbing."

The ladder Shaun had to climb extended from the control room, past a trap door, up the wall, and into the theater's hidden catwalks above. Employees used the walkways to change light bulbs in the massive chandeliers and once they were used in a production of *Aladdin.* A wire-strung magic carpet flew above the crowd with manikins dressed as the characters. That is until three performances into the run a manikin came loose and fell a hundred feet. Shaun wasn't in the theater that night but he'd heard that no one was hurt. The manikin, however, did not survive.

Shaun took a deep breath. If he could navigate the catwalks, moving above the zombees, he'd reach the emergency smoker tank, add Dr. Romero's new more potent solution, and then Toby could turn the smokers on. If everything went according to plan, this would be over in a few minutes. *Easy-peasy,* he thought.

"Okay," Shaun said, looking at Toby. He wondered if they should say goodbye or hug or something. It didn't seem very James Bond-like, but before he could make up his mind, Toby stuck out his hand. Shaun smiled and took it. "See you soon."

"Count on it, bro," Toby said.

Shaun started up the ladder running up the back wall.

"No stopping at the gift shop on the way," Toby said.

"Not planning on it." Shaun pressed against the door in the ceiling, pushed it open, and climbed up onto the roof of the control room. He needed to continue another thirty feet up the ladder before he'd reach the catwalk. He took a deep breath and kept climbing.

Toby's voice came over the headset. "Can you hear me?"

"Yeah," Shaun managed, panting.

"Dude, sounds like you're dying."

Shaun paused at the ladder's mid-point, his limbs shaking. "Remember all the times I climbed up the rope in gym class?"

"You've never made it up the rope."

Shaun took a deep breath. "Exactly."

"Hey, I don't mean to add to your drama, but the zombees are beginning to notice you."

Shaun looked down at hundreds of zombees, gazing up, pointing. Some jumped, as if trying to take flight, their paper maché, wire-and-felt wings flapping ridiculously.

"I'm not worried about them." Shaun turned back to the climb and eyed the catwalk. "Just keep an eye out for giant bees. If you see any of them heading my way—"

"Yeah, about them," Toby said.

"What?"

"I don't see them anymore."

"Wonderful," Shaun said, reaching the catwalk. He threw his leg over the railing and plopped down onto the metal gangway. He started trotting, slowly at first, but his confidence grew with each step. He glanced at the countdown. *Nine minutes. This is gonna be close.*

"Hey, I can see you," Toby said.

Shaun slowed to wave at Toby, or at least where Toby was. Shaun couldn't see through the tinted control room's windows.

"Hey, Shaun?" Toby said.

"What?"

"I didn't notice it before, but did you know your backpack is black?"

Shaun stopped at an intersection in the catwalk. "Yeah, so?"

"Isn't that one of the colors that the giant bees like to attack?"

"Fine time to tell me, dude." Shaun scanned ahead. The catwalk branched off and ran along the sides of the theater. Black curtains draped over the railing to hide it from theatergoers. He was just about to pick a direction when he heard a distant buzzing.

"Dude," Shaun said. "Do you see those bees anywhere?"

"No. Wait, I see two," Toby said. "They're down by the hive."

Earlier there were three, Shaun thought. *Where's the other one?* He looked ahead.

Shaun heard it again. Closer this time. His lungs began to tighten and he put a hand on his chest. *Not now. Please not now.* He unzipped a pocket and pulled out his inhaler. As he brought it to his lips, he heard the buzzing right behind him. He spun around so fast his hand smacked the rail. The inhaler tumbled from his grasp as a giant bee bore down on him. Shaun dropped to the metal floor and rolled onto his stomach. Something thumped his back, hard, as if the backpack had been punched.

The giant bee had plunged its stinger into the backpack and its frantic buzzing sounded like a siren. Thinking fast, he rolled onto his back. The buzzing turned to a sickening crunching sound. The back of Shaun's neck felt wet and he tried not to picture the insect's gross green ooze dripping down his back.

"Dude," Toby said. "Still no sign of that *third* bee."

Shaun sighed, and sat up. A piece of the squished bee's paper-thin wing fell into his lap. He grasped it between two fingers and flicked it over the rail to join his inhaler somewhere amongst the swarm of zombees below.

"Hey, Shaun," Toby said. "What're you doing sitting around? We only have seven minutes."

Shaun grabbed the rail and pulled himself up. His lungs felt good, almost as if he had used his inhaler. Moving again, he gazed at the area above the stage. He could make out the emergency smoker tank. It was big. A metal air duct rose up from it and fed into the ventilation system. "Almost there," he said.

"Okay," Toby said. "I'm going to power it up."

As Shaun neared the tank, a few red lights came to life on a panel next to several valves. He wasted no time and ran straight toward them. Sheriff Rosco said the tank's opening was next to the control panel. Shaun dropped the backpack and started unscrewing the tank's lid. It came off with a pop.

He set the lid down and pulled out the two canisters Dr. Romero had prepared. They looked like space-age drinking containers, milk cartons NASA might use on a future moon station.

"How's it going?" Toby said.

"I'm putting the first one in now."

"Looks like the system's all warmed up," Toby said, enthusiastically. "I think we're gonna make it."

The moment Toby's words ended, Shaun heard buzzing. His heart skipped a beat as he peered around. "Hey, Toby. Can you see those bees?"

"Just one," he said.

Shaun scanned up, then back behind him. He could hear the buzzing but couldn't see the source. He caught movement in his peripheral vision. The container in his hand had just emptied, and he swung it wildly at the shadow diving at him. There was a hollow thud as he smacked down the attacking bee with the empty container.

Five feet away and dazed, the bee struggled to right itself on the catwalk floor. Consumed with a rush of adrenalin, Shaun tossed the container and ran at the bee, yelling.

He kicked the bee so hard he almost lost his balance, but grabbed the rail. The giant bee's wings exploded from the impact. Its body launched up into the air, sailing toward two support beams in the catwalk that resembled goalposts. The now wingless insect tumbled end over end like a football right between the posts, then disappeared in the darkness.

Shaun threw his hand in the air, triumphantly. "Ha," he yelled. "Shouldn't play sports, my butt!"

"Dude, will you stop screwing around up there," Toby said. "We got like three minutes before the big boom."

"I'm on it." Shaun dashed back to the tank. He grabbed the final canister and dumped its contents into in the tank. Slapping the lid shut he said, "Okay, good to go." He looked down at his wristwatch. *Two minutes to spare.*

"Uh," Toby muttered.

"What's 'uh,' mean?" Shaun said.

"Something's not right. It says system not engaged."

"Well, engage it, man!"

"Just let me check the manual," Toby said. Shaun could hear him flipping pages. "I think I saw something about that."

Shaun eyed the countdown. *One minute, thirty seconds.* "I don't mean to rush you or anything, but—"

"Almost there," Toby said. "I think you need to—*AAAAH!*" Toby screamed so loud Shaun wanted to yank the headphones off.

"Toby, what's wrong?" Shaun heard a crash and sounds of a struggle. "Dude!"

"It's Sam," Toby finally answered. "She's awake!"

CHAPTER 22

"Bad, Sam!" Toby yelled. "Bad, Sam!"

"Are you okay?" Shaun said.

"The zombie suit saved my butt," Toby said. "Sam snuck up behind me and sunk her teeth into my shoulder."

"Where are you?"

"I'm on the control room roof. I think I'm safe. Zombees don't seem to be good climbers."

Shaun was relieved Toby was safe, but they had less than a minute left. "Did you bring the manual?"

"Yeah, yeah," Toby said, flipping pages. "Ah… system engage… Yes, here it is. Shaun, look for a lever on the tank near the main valve."

Shaun spotted a lever, half the size of a baseball bat, on the opposite side of the tank. "Got it!"

"Is it pointed up or down?"

"Up."

"You need—" Toby choked off suddenly.

"Toby! What do I need to do?"

"*Ahhhh*," Toby screamed.

"Dude!" Shaun heard Toby scrambling. "Are you okay?"

"Apparently Zombee-Sam is an excellent climber."

"What do I need to do?" Shaun repeated.

"The lever needs to point down. That should open the valve and release the smoke into the system."

Shaun was afraid of that. He had already noticed the catwalk didn't extend to the other side of the tank. There was another catwalk within easy reach of the lever, but he'd have to backtrack, and they were out of time. He needed to take the most direct route—climb up onto the tank and slide along its length.

As Shaun bounded up the rail, the sounds of scuffling boomed in his headset. It sounded like Toby was in a life and death struggle with Zombee-Sam, but there was nothing he could do for his friend. He looked down, immediately wishing he hadn't. He was over the zombee's hive. From this angle its honeycombed openings looked like an alien moonscape.

Shaun had nothing to hold onto as he scooted his body along the tank, but he managed to get within grabbing distance of the lever. He stretched, seized the handle, and pushed. It didn't move. He inched closer, grabbed it with both hands and pushed. Still, it would not budge.

"Toby, I can't move the handle."

"I got my own problems, dude," Toby shouted, sounding winded. "Put your weight into it—stop it Sam, stop it!"

Holding the lever tight, Shaun took a deep breath and slid down the side of the tank hoping the weight of his body would force the lever down. With no place to get a foothold, he slid free from the tank and dangled above the stage. The lever started to move, slowly arching downward. Shaun then realized that when it reached the down position, he would be unable to hold on. He'd slip right off.

The lever slammed down. As he began losing his grip, he heard the paralyzing smoke speeding through the ventilation system. Shaun smiled in relief—until a giant bee landed on his chest.

"You've got to be freaking kidding me!"

With the bee's stinger hovering over his abdomen, Shaun had no choice. He closed his eyes and let go of the lever.

Shaun blinked his eyes and tried to focus. His mind was running through images of a dream he'd just had in which he was falling. Suddenly realizing it wasn't a dream, he bolted upright, smacking his head into something wet and soft.

"Shaun, where are you, man?" Toby's voice sounded distant.

Shaun glanced down. The headphones were resting around his neck. He lifted them back on and said, "Toby, are you okay?"

"Yeah, I'm fine. Dude, where are you?"

Shaun looked around his confined area. He was surrounded by wet, slimy gunk. "I'm not sure." He peered up into the hole he'd created when he fell. He saw the massive smoker tank above. *If the tank is right above me,* he thought, *I must be in the hive!*

"Are you hurt?" Toby said.

"I don't think so." He stood up. A bee lay squashed underneath him. The bee and the enormous hive had broken his fall. Shaun slapped green bee-guts off his backside, then made his way to a honeycomb tunnel. "Hey, Toby, what happened to Sam? Did she bite you?"

"No, I managed to keep away from her, but man is she strong. I thought she was gonna pull my leg off."

Following his nose, Shaun turned a corner in the hexagon-shaped passage. "Where is she now?"

"She's asleep. Well, if you can call it sleep," Toby said. "They're all asleep. It's the world's biggest, creepiest slumber party out here."

Shaun trotted toward an opening. He stepped out onto the stage, surrounded by unconscious zombees. They were sprawled everywhere, two and three deep. They must have dropped right where they stood.

"Wow, Dr. Romero really knows his stuff," Shaun said.

"Yeah, well, let's not forget the part where this is all his fault."

Shaun checked his wristwatch. The countdown flashed *zero minus ten*, whatever that meant. "Do you think we made it in time?"

"No idea," Toby said. "I'm making my way to the lobby."

"See ya there, bro."

It took several minutes for Shaun to climb over the piles of unconscious zombees. At first he tried not to step on them, but it was taking forever, so after a few yards he started stone-stepping on top of them as Toby had earlier, doing his best James Bond from *Live and Let Die.*

When he made it to the lobby, Toby was already there, talking into his wristwatch.

"This is Toby, come in, Ellen."

"Any luck?" Shaun asked.

Toby shook his head. "Hey, M.I.G. dudes, we did it. All the zombees are neutered."

"Neutralized," Shaun corrected.

"What's the difference?" Toby said. "Nobody seems to be listening anyway."

Shaun pressed the gold button on his wristwatch. "Ellen, I hope you guys can hear us. The zombees are all asleep. I don't know for how long, but if you want to give everyone the antidote, now is the time."

Toby said, "Do you think they—"A thunderous roar boomed from outside. The boys exchanged dreadful glances, then turned to the lobby doors. The glass shook, but Shaun didn't think it was the bomb. He stepped over unconscious zombees and opened the doors.

Dawn had just broken, and Shaun raised a hand to block the glare. A hurricane of wind blasted in front of them, whipping debris all around. When his eyes adjusted, Shaun saw a helicopter landing in the street.

"Congratulations, boys," Ellen's voiced boomed through a megaphone. "You've done it."

CHAPTER 23

THE LIVING DAYLIGHTS

Three hours after Shaun had fallen into the monstrous beehive, he stood in the shadow of Major Captain.

The big man grinned ominously. "Thanks to you, we're gonna have to rewrite our protocols."

Shaun didn't know what else to say, so he said, "I'm sorry."

Major Captain reached into his pocket and pulled out a business card. "When you graduate high school, why don't you boys give us a call? There might be a place for you with M.I.G."

Shaun flipped the card over. It was blank on both sides. He handed it to Toby who flipped it as well. Before they could ask what the deal was, Major Captain turned on his heel and moved off. Filling the vacant space, Captain Major stepped close to the boys and pointed at their chests. "We'll be needing those suits back before we leave."

"I'll see to it, Captain Major," Ellen said, coming up behind them.

"See that you do," Captain Major said, then turned and followed Major Captain.

When he was far enough away, Shaun leaned toward Ellen. "Are you in a lot of trouble?"

"Yes and no," she said. "I'm in charge of coming up with the new rescue protocols for zombie outbreaks, which is good. But I did get demoted. I'm no longer Lieutenant Corporal. I'm Lieutenant Private, now."

"That doesn't sound so bad," Toby said.

"It's not," Ellen said. "Especially when you… oh, excuse me, guys."

Ellen moved past them and approached a young girl sitting up on a curb. It was Ellen's sister, Alice. Dr. Romero had administered the super-antidote to her and the young girl's eyes fluttered. She was one of three thousand just starting to wake up from their nightmare.

Shaun and Toby stood in a sea of people, all lying out on Main Street after being carried from the theater. There were several dozen full body bags filled with those to damaged physically too be helped. But the majority of Honeywell Springs' residents were slowly being brought back by Dr. Romero and an army of medical people, all wearing grey M.I.G. zombie suits. They moved about quickly, delivering the shots, one after the other. As people woke, they were escorted to a military truck, which would evacuate them to a camp just outside of town for further tests and observation. They'd be released in a few days, and thanks to Toby, Sam and Shaun, be able to come home to Honeywell Springs.

Ellen embraced her sister. Alice appeared groggy but hugged her older sibling back, enthusiastically. Shaun gazed at Alice, remembering how beautiful she was.

"Are you gonna go talk to her?" Toby said.

"Maybe later," Shaun said, feeling his cheeks blush.

"Dude, we just saved an entire town, maybe the world," Toby said. "What're you afraid of?"

Shaun smiled. "Fighting giant bees and the hordes of the undead is easy. But talking to girls. That's scary."

Toby laughed. "Well, there's no time like the present."

"The present for what?" Shaun said, but Toby was already walking away.

By the time he'd caught up, Toby was kneeling down next to Sam's body, resting on a stretcher. Sam had just received her shot and was trying to focus her eyes. Shaun knelt on the other side, and the boys watched as Sam came back to the world of the living.

"Oh, man. You guys are an ugly sight to wake up to."

Toby and Shaun chuckled.

Sam sat up and rubbed the shoulder where she received her shot. "So the super-antidote works, huh?"

"Thanks to my boy, Shaun here," Toby said.

Sam feigned disgust. "Does that mean I have dweeb blood in me?"

Shaun smiled. "One hundred percent, grade A dweeb blood. You should transform into a total dork within the hour."

Sam rolled her eyes. "Oh, well."

Shaun put a hand on Sam's shoulder. "I'm glad you're back, Sam."

"Me too," she said.

Toby turned to Shaun, his expression looking serious. "Hey, can you give us a minute?"

"Uh, sure," Shaun said. He stood and stepped away, but remained within earshot.

"How are you feeling, Sam?" Toby said.

"Fine," she replied. "But I don't remember anything after we made it to the control room. What happened after that?"

"Oh, Shaun made it to the tank, you tried to eat me," Toby said, waving his hand. "But it's not important. Look, they're gonna take you away in a minute and I need to ask you something."

Sam sat up further. "Okay."

"You know we've been through a lot tonight. Terror, adventure, a few near-death experiences, and I was just wondering, Sam…" Toby stammered. "If you… I mean… would you ever—"

Sam suddenly reached out, grabbed Toby's grey zombie suit, pulled him close and kissed him square on the mouth. After a few seconds she let Toby go and fell back onto the stretcher.

"Sam…" Toby managed.

Just then, two soldiers grabbed the handles of the stretcher and lifted Sam from the ground. As they started toward a truck, Sam narrowed her eyes at Toby. "If you tell anyone that happened, I'll tear your face off and use it as a Halloween mask."

Shaun walked back and stood next to Toby. "Yep, she's a real sweetheart." Shaun said. "I totally get why you like her."

Toby looked at Shaun with a goofy grin. "Did you see?"

Shaun slapped his back. "Sure did, bro. Even threw up in my mouth a little."

"Shaun, is that you?" said a grumpy voice from behind.

The boys spun around. Shaun's boss, Mr. Hooper was trying to sit up.

Shaun walked over to the big man. "How are you feeling, Mr. Hooper?"

"What happened," he barked. "How did I get here? Oh, my head?"

Shaun recalled whacking him with the golf club, and Sam running him down with the cart. "I think you hit your head, but you'll be okay," Shaun said, trying not to stare at the black tire tracks across his chest.

"Did you complete your delivery to Dr. Romero's?"

"No, sir." Shaun chuckled. "I got a little sidetracked."

"It'll come out of your wages, I'm afraid."

"That's ok, Mr. Hooper. I quit." Shaun grinned. "Life's too short to spend my summer delivering groceries, just so I can buy a video game."

Mr. Hooper looked like he was gonna blow his top, but before he could, Shaun turned away and rejoined Toby. The goofy grin was still plastered all over Toby's face, and it made Shaun smile.

"Shaun," Toby said. "Sam kissed me."

"Dude, I was there. It happened like a minute ago."

Toby's face went flush and his gaze fell to the ground. "Yeah, it did."

"Now if you can just keep her from beating you up."

"Don't move." Toby sounded alarmed.

Following Toby's gaze, Shaun looked down at a bumblebee crawling on his hand. How had he not noticed it landing? Now he could feel its legs moving over his knuckles. *It's so tiny.*

"Want me to get it?" Toby asked.

"I got this, dude," Shaun said. With his other hand, Shaun gently picked up the bee by the wings. He peered closely at the small creature. *They truly are amazing.* "Later days, little guy," Shaun said, then released the bee into the air.

Toby stared at Shaun, astonished.

"What?" Shaun said.

Toby shook his head and smiled. "Nothing, dude."

Then, as if it were something they did every day, they turned and strolled down Main Street, like they owned the town.

"So," Toby said. "Do you think you might actually come to next years Founder's Day Festival?"

"Nah," Shaun said. "After this one, all future festivals will seem kind of boring, don't you think?"

Toby put an arm around his friend. "So true, bro. So very true."

DR. MAX ROMERO'S
CREEPY BUT COOL BEE FACTS

Cannibalism

When supplies are scarce, bees are known to turn to the only food source available – *each other*. Bees will eat their hive mates and larvae when times get tough.

Undertakers

When bees die within the colony, workers collect the dead bodies and act like undertakers, removing the corpses from the hive. They also act as security, ejecting the sick and any unneeded males during times of famine.

Deadly Mating

Mating rituals are gruesome for male bees. Drone bees, whose sole purpose is to fertilize the queen, suffer the traumatic loss of their reproductive organ which remains inside the queen. With their abdomens torn open, the male drones quickly die. Even if they should survive, wounded drones are ejected from the hive by the undertakers.

Bug Eyes

Bees have five eyes; two large compound eyes on the side of their head and three small ocelli eyes in the center of their head to help with flight navigation. They also have hair on their eyes!

Killer Bees

Africanized bees (or Killer Bees) are man made! Warwick E. Kerr created them in the 1950s by crossing a European bee with an African bee. He hoped to make a bee that could live in the jungle. He got a bee that swarms by the hundreds of millions, is insanely territorial, mindlessly aggressive, and has killed at least 1,000 people in the Americas.

World Record Number of Stings

Although a man in Nevada claimed to have been stung over 3,000 times, no official number was ever tabulated. According to the Guinness Book of World Records the greatest number of bee stings sustained by any surviving human is 2,443 by Johannes Relleke at the Kamativi tin mine, Gwaii River, Wankie District, Zimbabwe (then Rhodesia) on January 28, 1962. All the stings were removed and counted. OUCH!

Zom*BEEs*

ZomBees are bees that have been parasitized by the zombie fly, *Apocephalus borealis*. Female flies lay their eggs in the bee, and as the larvae develop, they attack the bee's brain, muscles and nervous system. Infected bees can be found walking in circles as well as losing the ability to stand. Fly-parasitized bees are called "zombees" because they show the "zombie-like behavior" of leaving their hives at night in a disoriented state. The bees will also remain inactive during the daytime until death occurs. The mature fly will typically emerge from their bee host between the head and thorax. Nasty!

ABOUT THE AUTHOR

Kevin David Anderson is a former marketing and public relations professional turned fiction writer. His short stories have appeared in the pages of Dark Animus, Dark Wisdom, Darkness Rising, Dark Moon Digest, and a bunch of other publications with the word *dark* in the title. His stories are also available in audio, on podcasts like the Dunesteef, Pseudopod and the Drabblecast. Anderson is the creator and co-author of the novel *Night of the Living Trekkies*, published by Quirk Books. He lives and writes in Southern California and you can find him at: www.KevinDavidAnderson.com

Also by
KEVIN DAVID ANDERSON

Night of the Living Trekkies

From Quirk Books - Journey to the final frontier of sci-fi zombie horror! A zombie parasite from space infects a Star Trek convention and its up to Jim Pike and his ragtag crew of fanboys and fangirls to find a way to survive. But how long can they last in the ultimate no-win scenario?

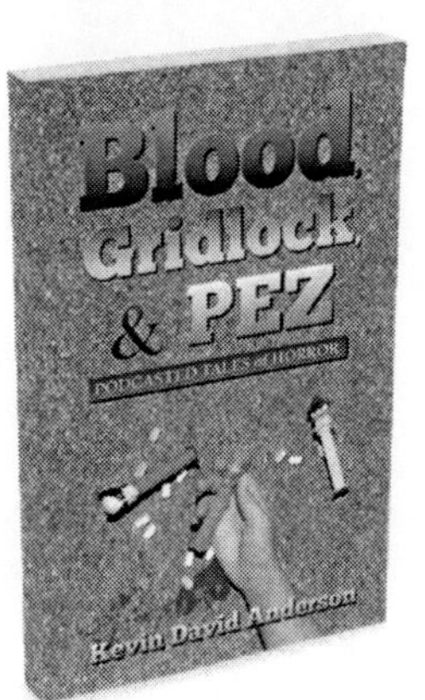

Blood, Gridlock, & PEZ
Podcasted Tales of Terror

Visit a post apocalyptic world where it becomes difficult to distinguish friends from food. Summon nerves of steel to remove the spiders living in a human brain. Conspire with malevolent jack-o'-lanterns to stop a madman. And stand up to death in the middle of a traffic jam with only your wits, and PEZ.

ACKNOWLEDGEMENTS

I'd like to thank Amber Jacques for sparking the idea, my editor Lee Allen Howard, my father for his extra set of eyes, Peachtree Publishers' Helen Harriss and Chronicle Books' editor Ariel Richardson for their insightful suggestions, Bo Kaier for his amazing cover art, Rish Outfield for making the audiobook sound fantastic, and most of all I'd like to thank my wife and family who make all the wonderful things in my life possible.

Sir Connery's

HONEYDOGS

HUNNY

Made in
Honeywell Springs
since 1962

CPSIA information can be obtained at www.ICGtesting.com
Printed in the USA
LVOW11s1917310716

R11183100001B/R111831PG498465LVX1B/1/P